"IF YOU THINK I'VE COME OUT WEST TO GET LASSOED BY SOME TWO-BIT PHONY COWBOY LIKE YOU, YOU'RE SADLY MISTAKEN."

Bree continued, "I'm here for one reason, and one reason only: business."

"You've made that point already," Will told her.

"Well, I hope so. I suppose I've gone and bruised that sensitive ego of yours, but I happen to believe in being honest. And the truth is, you simply don't make it in my book as a cowboy Casanova."

He gave her an angry look, then gripped her shoulders and pulled her close to him. "Let me tell you something, Bree Winston. You talk about phonies—well, you take the cake. You are as phony as they come, sweetheart. If I know one thing, I know when a woman's appetites are sparked. And like it or not, Bree, I spark yours—and you can't deny it."

CANDLELIGHT ECSTASY CLASSIC ROMANCES

WILD SURRENDER

Alison Tyler

A CANDLELIGHT ECSTASY ROMANCE®

Published by
Dell Publishing Co., Inc.
1 Dag Hammarskjold Plaza
New York, New York 10017

ISBN: 0-440-19531-4

Printed in the United States of America

August 1987

10 9 8 7 6 5 4 3 2 1

WFH

To Our Readers:

We have been delighted with your enthusiastic response to Candlelight Ecstasy Romances®, and we thank you for the interest you have shown in this exciting series.

In the upcoming months we will continue to present the distinctive sensuous love stories you have come to expect only from Ecstasy. We look forward to bringing you many more books from your favorite authors and also the very finest work from new authors of contemporary romantic fiction.

As always, we are striving to present the unique, absorbing love stories that you enjoy most—books that are more than ordinary romance. Your suggestions and comments are always welcome. Please write to us at the address below.

Sincerely,

The Editors
Candlelight Romances
1 Dag Hammarskjold Plaza
New York, New York 10017

WILD SURRENDER

CHAPTER ONE

Grace Adams sighed dramatically, letting a thin stream of smoke drift out of her delicately pouting lips. She took another long drag of her cigarette before dousing it, then regarded her friend Bree Winston with a sympathetic half smile. "You poor darling," she said.

"Accent on the poor," Bree muttered, noting that Grace's smile also held a touch of triumph. Bree shrugged. Let Grace have her day. After all, for three years Grace's smiles had been tinged with envy. For three years, Bree Winston had had it all: money, jewels, status, and a very rich, very successful husband.

She stared around the large empty bedroom of her Manhattan penthouse. Her toes were making a series of small dents in the plush cinnamon-colored carpet. It was the only evidence remaining of the elegant furnishings that had once filled the lavish quarters; the rest of it had been reclaimed late that morning.

Grace took hold of Bree's hand and examined her fingers. "Why, the bastard even demanded his rings back!"

Bree pulled her hand away. "I threw them at him."

"Bree, really. That temper of yours has always gotten you into trouble. I know it's pointless to rehash the whole thing—"

"Absolutely pointless," Bree emphasized, even though she knew it was also pointless to try to stop Grace from speaking her mind.

"But I do believe," Grace went on, true to form, "that your marriage was doomed from the first. You and James could never see eye to eye on anything."

"Especially not on his 'eye' for the ladies." Bree brushed back her hair, the color of which bore a remarkable similarity to the cinnamon carpet. She normally wore it loose to her shoulders in an orderly tumble, but it was less orderly now that she could no longer afford to have Henri from Antoine's, the elite hair emporium, drop in once a week to tame it into obedience. She plucked a silk scarf out of her open suitcase and tied it rather ruthlessly around her wild locks.

"Your first mistake was agreeing to sign that insane prenuptial contract," Grace went on, wanting to focus her heart-to-heart on Bree's shortcomings rather than on James's. No point bad-mouthing the man who just happened to be, as of yesterday's final divorce decree, one of the most eligible bachelors in town, she thought. And if the opportunity arose, Grace would certainly know how to handle a man like James Winston—unlike Bree, who, despite her appearance of chic sophistication, was really quite naïve—and,

Grace further suspected, foolishly romantic, although Bree would certainly have denied that adamantly.

Bree snapped the lock on her suitcase and slipped her stockinged feet into a pair of navy leather pumps. "The first mistake I made regarding my ex-husband was marrying him."

"But what will you do now, darling?" Grace persisted, watching Bree stand up and brush the creases off her pale blue Anne Klein silk shantung suit. At least she still had her extravagant wardrobe. Grace supposed James wouldn't be passing out used garments to his current lady friends, although she was certain Bree's elegant jewels would soon bedeck some of the loveliest necks, wrists, and fingers in town. Loath as she was to admit it, she couldn't imagine those jewels looking better on anyone than they did on her exquisite friend Bree.

Not only was Bree Winston beautiful, she handled that beauty with the nonchalance of someone who had lived with beauty all her life. No one feature in her delicately shaped oval face was a real standout; all the parts formed what would have to be described as a perfect whole. There were the high cheekbones, the full mouth, the patrician nose, the heavy thick slash of brows, and those brilliant aquamarine eyes that radiated a sultry heat and that were trimmed with an extravagant curling of thick lash.

Bree wasn't tall, no more than five six, but her thin, graceful body and her proud carriage created the illusion of height. And here, too, all the parts fit together to perfection. Not only was she blessed with a figure that held not the slightest lump of fat, but she didn't have to spend endless hours working out at an exclusive gym to achieve her shape, either. That didn't mean she eschewed working out, but for Bree it was purely a social form of recreation. Like all her chic friends, Bree belonged to the classiest gym in town— or had, until her annual membership dues had come up for renewal last month. It was one more extravagance that now had to fall by the wayside.

"Bree," Grace said, her voice more strident, "you need a sensible plan of action."

Bree smiled sardonically. She gave the bedroom a final sweeping glance, then focused her attention on her attractive blond friend. "I do have a plan, Grace. You simply don't approve of it."

"Bree, you're crazy!"

"Maybe. But practical."

"Practical!" Grace screeched, a hint of a Brooklyn accent sneaking unbidden into her voice. "You call flying off to some godforsaken town in Wyoming and taking over a fleabag rodeo practical?"

Bree lifted her heavy suitcase with effort. The two clothing trunks filled with the rest of her possessions had already been picked up. "I'm not flying, Grace. I can't afford those frivolous extravagances anymore. I've got better things to do with the money I managed to save over the past few years. I'm taking the train, remember? So how about giving me the lift to Penn Station that you promised?" She walked with long strides to the bedroom door and paused when she got there. "And it isn't a rodeo, Grace, darling. It's a Wild West show."

Grace rushed over to Bree and grabbed her arm. "Darling, listen to me. Don't you realize, you idiot, that James handed you that—that ridiculous investment as a further slap in the face? He told you himself that he'd picked up that has-been troupe as a tax dodge. He needed a big loss, and he got it."

Bree pulled her arm away, and her aquamarine eyes took on a frosty hue. "I know exactly what James had in mind, Grace, when he so generously gave me ownership of that troupe. Which is precisely why I intend to get in the last slap."

"And just how do you propose to do that?"

"By turning that has-been troupe of cowboys and cowgirls into a first-class money-making extravaganza."

"And how do you plan to manage that? Since when do you know anything about the Wild West, darling? The farthest west you've ever been is Aspen, Colorado, for a luxury ski vacation."

"I may not know anything about the wild and woolly West, but I do know that a little glitz and a sprinkling of glamour can go a long way," Bree said, eyeing Grace pointedly. "And I figure those cowpokes out in Ritter Creek, Wyoming, have got to be bone-weary of being a losing proposition. I'm sure they'll be eager to have a real owner show some serious interest in turning their fortunes around."

13

Grace raised one carefully plucked brow and shook her head slowly, giving Bree one of her sublimely rueful gazes. "Well, darling, all I can say is, good luck." She made no effort to disguise the facetious tone in her voice.

Bree grinned. "Thanks, Grace. I knew you'd wish me well."

Bree Winston was full of high spirits as the train pulled out of Penn Station. They lasted clear through to New Jersey. Over the rest of what felt like an endless trek across wheat fields, plains, and more wheatfields, her spirits sank drastically with each successive mile. By the time the train pulled into the Green River, Wyoming, station, Bree was sorely regretting her foolish decision. Much as she hated to admit it, she knew Grace was right. What, indeed, did she know about the West? More to the point, what in God's name did she know about Wild West shows?

She glanced around the wooden platform, empty save for a tired-looking stationmaster who was sitting on a chair tilted precariously against the wall of the depot house, reading the paper. She'd been the only passenger to alight at Green River. No wonder, she concluded, her gaze shifting from the wooden depot house to the harsh, barren fields of sagebrush that stretched out beyond the station. The monotony of the landscape was broken here and there only by jagged outcroppings of sandstone. Beyond were low brown hills, and farther in the distance Bree could make out a string of purple mountains that she supposed were part of the Rocky Mountain range. Overhead, the late afternoon sky was washed-out blue, uninterrupted by clouds. It was more sky than Bree could remember seeing.

For reasons she couldn't fathom, it felt ominous. In fact, the entire western landscape that swept around her felt eerie and disturbingly alien. So this was springtime in the Rockies! Not quite what she had imagined. Then again, she hadn't let herself imagine too much about her new surroundings or her new adventure. If she had, she might never have come out here. In fact, had there been a train pulling out of the station heading east at that precise moment, Bree Winston might just have hopped right on it.

Then again, she might not. There was nothing back east for her anymore. Only a few friends who eyed her with pity and told her how crummy it was that she couldn't make it to the gym anymore, or afford the fancy "ladies' " lunches. Or the weekly—sometimes daily—shopping sprees. No, there was nothing back east for her. The truth was, there hadn't been much there for the past two years. That was when her marriage had really started to fall apart. After months of seesawing back and forth between separations and reconciliations, she'd finally filed for a divorce.

To file for divorce hadn't been an easy decision for Bree. Not that there was any love left between her and James. That had died a long time ago. But there was the matter of their prenuptial agreement: If she filed for divorce, it meant she would lose everything. Bree was used to luxury. She accepted it with the same nonchalance with which she accepted her beauty. Giving it all up wasn't easy. But in the end she came to the conclusion that giving up her pride and independence would be tougher than giving up the ample creature comforts that James's money had provided.

Besides, she thought, wiping her brow of a bead of perspiration, there was the Sheridan Wild West Show to hang her hopes and dreams on. And to throw herself into. She needed a project, something real, something that could honestly matter to her. Bree felt it vital to make a success of this enterprise. She needed to prove her worth, not simply to get the last laugh on James. Bree needed to prove to herself that she could make it on her own.

She set down her heavy suitcase and walked with purposeful strides over to the stationmaster, who went on reading the paper as she approached. She cleared her throat.

"Excuse me," she said politely.

The stationmaster didn't look up.

"Excuse me." This time her tone held a touch of irritation. "Is there a cab stand around here? I need to get to Ritter Creek."

"Ritter Creek? What for?" The stationmaster lifted his eyes upward without moving his drooped head. "Ain't much happenin' in Ritter Creek."

Didn't she know it!

"Nevertheless, I am going there." There was a note

16

of defiance in Bree's voice. It was a dangerous quality of hers, this compulsion to buck the odds. Look where it had gotten her—marriage to James Harley Winston. All she had to show for her three years of wedded "bliss" was a divorce decree and the ownership of a down-at-the-heels Wild West troupe.

The stationmaster shielded his eyes from the glaring sun and studied her more closely. "Ritter Creek, huh?"

Bree bit down on her lower lip. "Ritter Creek."

"And you want a cab."

"Don't tell me Green River still relies on stage-coaches."

He chuckled. "We don't rely much on cabs, I'll tell you that."

"Then how do you propose I travel to Ritter Creek?" Bree glared at the stationmaster as she swiped at a bead of sweat that was running down her cheek.

The lean, hawk-nosed man's smile grew wry as he glanced down at Bree's crumpled suit. "Well, now, you could give Bill Unger a jingle."

"Bill Unger?"

"He's got a station wagon that he uses to take some of the old folks over to the shopping center in town, and when they need it, he gives them lifts over to the health clinic in Rock Springs."

"You mean he runs a cab service." Bree's voice was sharp. She had the distinct feeling the stationmaster was intentionally putting her on.

His sly smile confirmed her impression. So much for western hospitality.

"Is there a phone I can use?"

The stationmaster looked off toward the road, not answering her right off.

"Surely you have a phone inside." Her tone was strident. She pulled her suit jacket closed. In a matter of minutes, it felt as if the temperature had dropped twenty degrees. Her white silk shirt, which had been damp with perspiration, now made her skin feel cold and clammy.

"Won't be needing Unger, so it seems."

Bree's eyes narrowed in puzzlement. Then she followed the stationmaster's gaze. She shielded her own eyes from the setting sun as an old Jeep rounded the bend of the road.

"Who's that?" she queried as the Jeep drew up to the station.

Bree wasn't surprised when she didn't receive an answer. Or maybe she had but was too distracted to hear the stationmaster's response. Almost hypnotically, all her attention was suddenly riveted on the tall, dark cowboy who was swinging his powerfully built frame out of the Jeep.

The way he moved reminded Bree of the way a film cowboy riding into some bandit-riddled western town dismounted from his steed. There was a potent air of a man expecting trouble—or possibly looking for it. Whichever, the man damned well looked as if he could handle anything that came up.

The stranger approached slowly, walking with a tiger's sway that exuded pure masculinity. He was dressed in a dark blue shirt, well-worn jeans, a sheepskin-lined leather vest, and a felt cowboy hat. The dusty brim was pulled low over his eyes. The only items missing from the role of Bree's imaginary movie star cowboy were spurs attached to beautifully tooled leather boots, a gun holster strapped provocatively low, and two six-shooters decorating each narrow hip.

When he halted directly in front of her, Bree's heart stopped. Even without the guns this man could put many a film star to shame. He'd tilted his hat up an inch so that she could look up into the most searing sky-blue eyes she'd ever seen. Unthinkingly, she found herself staring unabashedly directly into them.

His hands rested lightly on his hips. Bree expected the cowboy to say something very "western," like, "Trouble, ma'am? Reckon I can be of some service." His voice would be low-pitched, and it would ring with seductive amusement.

Instead the cowboy shook his head slowly, the expression on his craggy face one not of amusement but of irritation. "That husband of yours warned me you might come sashaying out here. I told him you'd have to be plumb loco." His voice was low-pitched, but there was no humor or seduction in his tone. He paused; his bold blue eyes looked straight into her startled gaze. "You know what your hubby answered me? He said, 'Man, you hit the nail right on the head.' "

Bree felt a flash of rage, but when she opened her mouth to speak, no sound came.

Her lack of voice didn't seem to trouble the cowboy in the least. He leaned toward her, one arm extended. Bree drew back instantly, her blue-green eyes darkening.

"I suppose you won't be happy till you see the whole shootin' match for yourself," he went on, taking another step toward her and grabbing her arm despite her efforts to repel him.

Bree stared at him, incensed. Yet as angry as she was at this total stranger who was clasping her wrist with a firm, no-nonsense hold, she was unable to ignore the strong muscles that moved beneath the sleeves of his taut cotton shirt. His other hand reached down and lifted her suitcase.

She stood her ground as he tried to steer her toward the Jeep.

"Do you mind telling me who the hell you are?" she demanded, finally finding her voice, although it came out huskier than usual.

The man's fingers loosened their grip on her arm slightly; his finely shaped mouth curved into a faint smile. "Why, I'm the star of the show, ma'am. I'm Will Sheridan, the roughest, toughest sharpshooter this side of the Pecos." He glanced over his shoulder at the stationmaster, who'd blithely gone back to reading his paper. "Ain't that right, Andy?" the cowboy drawled.

Andy didn't look up from his paper, but he chuckled with clear amusement. "You're the best there is, Sheridan."

Bree didn't doubt it, although the stationmaster's confirmation only added to her present fury. "I'll decide that for myself," she said coolly.

Will Sheridan chuckled softly. His blue eyes insolently drifted down her body, making a slow, provocative appraisal. "I like a woman who makes her own decisions—within reason, of course."

The stationmaster found Will's tag line tremendously amusing and broke out into a hearty guffaw. He even abandoned his paper for a minute to share his laugh with the cowboy.

Bree glared at both men in turn, wrenching her suitcase from Sheridan's hand. He didn't put up a struggle, even though the suitcase was extremely heavy.

She started off for the Jeep, feeling ridiculous as her bag slammed into her thigh with each awkward step. The feeling only mounted as she grappled with the case, lifting it up into the rear of the open Jeep. When she looked back over her shoulder, she saw Will Sheridan exactly where she'd left him. He'd pulled out a small leather pouch and was slowly, casually rolling himself a smoke. He stood shooting the breeze with the stationmaster.

Bree had never met a more insufferable man. Maybe he did look good enough to stick up on the silver screen, but as far as manners or even the slightest hint of class went, Will Sheridan was a total zero. Oh, she knew what he was up to, all right. It didn't take any great genius to figure that out. He didn't like the idea of a woman coming out to run the operation. No, he didn't like that one little bit.

"Well," Bree muttered under her breath as she watched him amble over to the Jeep, "like it or not, he's stuck with me."

She had climbed into the Jeep before Will Sheridan got to her side. Not that she expected anything so gallant as his helping her in. Quite the contrary—she wouldn't put it past the man to hop right into his Jeep and take off, leaving her standing there in a cloud of dust.

Bree sat primly as Will hoisted himself up into the driver's seat. He glanced over at her. She had her arms clasped across her chest, and she was trying hard not to shiver as the setting sun drifted down over the distant mountains.

"You're going to be mighty chilly riding in this open Jeep," he commented dryly as he pulled out. "It's a good hour's ride to the ranch."

"I'll be fine," she said archly.

"No coat, huh?"

Bree didn't answer. Actually, she did have a fox jacket in her suitcase, but she knew she would look absolutely ridiculous arriving at the ranch in furs. The designer suit was bad enough. Besides, she didn't want to give Will, or any of the other members of the troupe, the idea that she was rolling in money. She wanted them to see her as one of them. She wanted them to realize that it was as much in her interest to turn their show into a first-class operation as it was in theirs.

They drove in silence for a while. Bree didn't say anything for fear he'd hear her teeth chattering. Will seemed totally self-contained. No doubt he was a man of few words; the few he'd offered so far didn't rank high in Bree's estimation. For the most part she kept her eyes focused straight ahead, but every now and then she cast a surreptitious glance over at Will. Despite the chilly winds, he seemed unbothered by the cold. His shirt sleeves were rolled up just below the elbows, and Bree was again sharply aware of the well-defined muscles pressing against the fabric of his shirt.

He turned his head once in her direction, and their eyes met for a brief instant. Bree's breath caught. She'd never encountered a man so magnetically masculine. She pulled her eyes away as she noted the subtle sneer in those full, sensuous lips that gave his expression a ruthless look. Bree sensed at that instant that Will Sheridan could be a dangerous man.

"I liked your husband," Will said, breaking the long silence. His comment was so out of the blue that Bree turned to face him with a startled look in her eyes.

"I didn't think you knew him well enough to have formed an opinion."

Will grinned. "That's why I liked him. Or I should say, I liked the way he ran the show." There was a brief pause. "He never got involved," he added pointedly.

"He ran our marriage the same way," Bree said

dryly. "And for the record, Mr. Sheridan, James Winston is not my husband any longer. So I'd appreciate it if you'd stop referring to him in that fashion."

Will glanced over at her for a moment but said nothing. A few minutes later he abruptly slowed the Jeep and turned into the parking lot of a quaint log-style roadside tavern. "Come on. You need a drink to warm up."

Bree hesitated. A drink in a cozy-looking bar sounded good, but she wasn't sure she wanted to sit face-to-face with Will Sheridan over cocktails before she'd steeled herself against his rough-hewn appeal.

He laughed softly, leaning toward her. "Hey, you did come out here to drown your sorrows over your divorce, didn't you? Might as well start now. The sooner you do, the quicker you'll get it out of your system."

If he'd expected his remark to spark her outrage, he got himself one hell of a surprise. Instead of sputtering in fury, Bree broke out into honey-toned laughter. "Drown my sorrows!" she gasped between giggles. "Is that what James told you? That I was coming out here to try to get over him? Of course you believed him without a second thought. You would. You men are all alike."

Will's eyes darkened. "Then why the hell did you come?" he barked, clearly irritated at her response.

Bree's laughter vanished. She turned to Will, her lips tightening to a line. "You need my help," she said solemnly.

Now it was Will's turn to burst out into laughter. When he got it under control, he let his eyes rake over her once more. This time there was no mistaking the insolently seductive inspection. "So I need your help, do I?" His lips twisted into a wry grin. "Well, now," he drawled, "I suppose you do have—a thing or two— to offer a man. Must admit, it gets kind of lonely out on the ranch rehearsing all the time for the summer tour. A man does get a little thirsty for something new and exciting."

Bree pulled herself up stiffly. "Your wit, Mr. Sheridan, is exceeded only by your acumen in show business. I'd say they're both in a sorry state and could use all the help they can get. I'm afraid you'll have to struggle with your wit—and your thirsts—on your own. The only help I'm here to give you is with your Wild West Show."

Bree's jaw muscles tightened as he stared silently at her. At least he wasn't laughing. Before he'd started telling her she didn't know the first thing about running a Wild West show, she admitted as much.

"But," she went on firmly, "I do have some ideas— some good ideas," she added for emphasis. "Anyway," she said, taking a deep breath, "I can't do much worse than James. I intend to do better—much better."

She took another breath, waiting for Will Sheridan's reaction. She found his unreadable expression most disturbing. She was well aware that without his cooperation she was going to have a rough time of it. As those sensuous blue eyes of his held her gaze, she suddenly realized, with a disturbing rush of arousal, that she was going to have a rough time getting cooperation. As insufferable and self-satisfied as she found Will Sheridan, there was no denying that the man did have a raw animal appeal.

She turned away from him, quickly getting down from the Jeep. "Well," she said, her voice a little shaky, "now that that's settled, I could use that drink." Her aquamarine eyes sparkled as he drew up beside her. "And since I don't have any sorrows to drown, Mr. Sheridan, maybe we can drink to success." Her tone held a questioning note.

Will Sheridan's dark brows quirked up as he cast her a long, intense look. Finally he murmured in his low drawl, "Maybe we can—ma'am."

There was something in that look, something in the deep, resonant tone of his voice, that made Bree realize that they were not within light-years of striking a bargain. Yet annoyed as she was by what she was certain Will Sheridan meant by *success,* a high color rose in her cheeks, and there was a most disturbing fluttering sensation in the pit of her stomach.

CHAPTER TWO

"Is Will Sheridan your real name or your stage name?" Bree eyed him questioningly after taking a couple of warming sips of Scotch.

"It's a name." Will was drinking whiskey, a double, straight up.

"It's polite to give a straight answer to a straight question," Bree said, irritated by Sheridan's frustrating style of repartee. "Unless there's some reason—"

"I reckon it's as real as any," he said, his blue eyes openly amused.

"You don't offer much, do you?" She took another swallow of Scotch, aware, even as she cast her eyes down, that Sheridan was smiling broadly.

"I thought you were the one here offering me . . ." He paused, his eyes glinting seductively. "What was it you were goin' to offer me, ma'am? Some good ideas, wasn't it?"

Bree glared at him. "I don't find you or your phony western twang the least bit amusing."

"Didn't know that was what I was supposed to be doing . . . ma'am."

Bree felt her cheeks growing warm. Never in her life had she run across a man who behaved so insufferably toward her. Men usually fell all over themselves trying to win her interest and attention. But while Will Sheridan made no bones about indicating that he found her sexually attractive, he certainly didn't know anything about bedding a woman of her character and breeding.

Bree's cheeks flushed more deeply at her musings. To bed, indeed! The last place in the world she planned to end up was in Will Sheridan's bed. Even if he did have a certain untamed sexual appeal, Bree found his cocky manner infuriating. Why, even if she'd found him irresistible, she'd never consider giving him the satisfaction of the win. And that, she was convinced, was exactly how he would see it. She was certain that this dark, compelling cowboy was as used to getting his way with women as she was with men. Well, maybe they had both met their match.

"Want another drink?" Will asked.

Bree set down her empty glass and shook her head slowly. She looked across the booth at Will, her expression softening. She knew she was going to get nowhere by continuing this verbal shooting match with Will Sheridan. For one thing, he was too good at it. For another, like it or not, she needed his cooperation.

"I gather you've pretty much been running this Wild West show on your own up to now." Bree made every effort to give her tone an understanding note.

Will tipped the brim of his cowboy hat back on his head, giving Bree a clearer glimpse of his thick, dark brown hair while the soft light in the tavern illuminated his hard-edged, square-jawed, deeply tanned face.

Even when Will smiled, as he was doing now, there was an uncompromising toughness about his features. The crease lines highlighted the corners of his eyes and mouth, emphasizing a raw, unyielding stubbornness.

"Look," Bree went on, trying to spark some sympathy in Will, "I'm not your enemy. It's as important to me as it is to you to see the Sheridan Wild West Show flourish. Are you too stubborn and chauvinistic to see that we both want the same thing?"

A muscle jerked in Will's cheek as he studied her face. "How do you know what I want?" he asked in that deep, resonant voice of his.

Surprisingly, there was no belligerence in his tone, not even annoyance. Bree couldn't figure out what Will was feeling. That baffled her. She'd been certain that Will Sheridan was a man easily figured out. Now she wasn't so sure.

She stared at him. There was a long silence, but this time Bree didn't feel awkward and uncomfortable as she had during the silences while they drove here. The truth was, Bree wasn't any surer about what she was feeling at that moment than she was about what made a man like Will Sheridan tick.

Finally, she said in a muted voice. "I guess I don't know what you want, Mr. Sheridan. But I do know what I want."

The enigmatic expression faded from Will's face; his

lips curved into a broad smile. "And I reckon you're a lady used to getting what you want."

Bree leaned slightly forward. "I don't always get everything I want. I wanted a happily-ever-after marriage, for instance. I most certainly didn't get that. But you know something, Mr. Sheridan? Losing every now and then can spark a person's motivation. Right now, Mr. Sheridan, you are looking at a woman who is very motivated and very determined." She drew the tip of her tongue along her dry lips and waited for what she was certain would be a snappy come-back line.

Once again Will surprised her. His broad smile turned tender. "I can see that, Miss Bree Winston. And I'm not saying I don't like what I see."

"Well." Bree smiled back, unaware that her smile was beguilingly girlish and most outstandingly alluring. "I guess that's a start."

Will reached across and touched her hand briefly. "I guess it is . . . ma'am," he answered with a wink, well aware from the shimmering look in Bree Winston's aquamarine eyes that his touch had had its desired effect.

During the rest of the drive out to Ritter Creek, Bree felt much more relaxed. She asked Will questions about the Wild West show: how many were in the troupe, what kind of acts there were, where they performed, how the performances were arranged. She didn't ask about how they did financially. She already knew that: miserably. The backwater towns the show appeared in brought in small audiences with little money. Profits were not something the Sheridan Wild West Show had had to bother themselves with—yet.

Will, true to form, answered her questions tersely. All she learned was that there were anywhere from seven to ten people in the troupe, depending on the weather, God, and how many bars there were in the town they happened to be performing in at any given time.

"Besides," Will added dryly, "can't say as the pay inspires devotion to the show. Although I've got five or six dedicated showmen. Pardon me, ma'am—that's show people, I mean. You being a liberated woman and all, I guess I'll be having to watch the way I speak to you."

Bree grinned. "I've just begun to taste liberation, Mr. Sheridan. And I may as well warn you, I like it. But for more reasons than that, cowboy, I do think you'd do well to watch the way you speak to me."

Will laughed. "Yes, ma'am."

"Which includes," Bree said firmly, "not calling me ma'am. After all, Mr. Sheridan, we have come a long way from the untamed frontier days of the Wild West."

Will made a sharp turn onto a deeply rutted dirt road, causing both the Jeep and Bree to take several hefty bounces. "Well, now, I'd wait awhile if I were you before saying that with so much conviction, ma'am—I mean, Ms. Winston."

Bree could see what Will meant. They rounded the bend past a series of open corrals on either side of the dirt road up to the heart of the Circle S Ranch, a low-slung building of rough-hewn logs and a cedar-shingled roof that looked as if it had seen better days—a good seventy-five years ago. A thick cloud of smoke rose from the center chimney, and a faint sound of music wafted through the smoke-scented air. Country music. Much like the kind Bree imagined they used to play at church socials when the West was just getting settled. She shot a wry smile over to Will as he pulled up the emergency brake a few yards from the house.

"How . . . western," she said dryly. "Are we in time for the square dance?"

Will merely grinned. "Guess the gang's all there. I'd better warn you, there's a few of them in there who'll be calling you ma'am who won't be able to break the habit too easily."

"I won't be too hard on them—at first," Bree announced airily, wishing, as she extricated herself from the Jeep, that she could have done so with a little more grace.

She started for the front door with a determined step. Bree wasn't expecting any warmer a reception from the rest of the troupe than she'd gotten from Will, but she felt more prepared for them, thanks to the cowboy.

"Hey, what about your gear?" Will called out, one hand resting idly on the roll bar of the Jeep. "I know how you liberated women like to pull your own weight." He gave her another of his slow, provocative appraisals.

This time Bree refused to rise to the bait. She was sure Will was trying to get her riled so that she'd make a bad impression on the "gang," as he called them. Well, she was not about to lose her cool now.

"Would you be so kind, Mr. Sheridan, as to bring my suitcase in for me?" She smiled saccharinely. "Please."

"Well now, ma'am"—Will grinned—"I reckon I can manage that for you."

Bree did a mock curtsey and then turned, waiting for Will to catch up to her.

"This place sure does need some tender loving care," she commented after she nearly fell through a rotting tread on her way up to the porch. "I can't believe James didn't even lay out a few bucks to make this place livable. Well"—she bypassed a gaping hole in the wooden porch—"I won't be able to put too much of my savings into the ranch itself, but I am going to see to it that a person doesn't kill herself just trying to make it to the front door."

When she finished that speech, she was almost at the door, and saw Will's hand snake out and grab her arm roughly. She looked into his darkened face with shocked surprise.

"For the record, Ms. Winston, your hubby bought control only of the Sheridan Wild West Show, not of this place. The ranch did not belong to your husband. So it does not belong to you now, either. Therefore, if you have any—complaints—about the place, you'll have to take them up with the owner of the Circle S. The sole owner."

"Meaning you," Bree said, wincing in pain as she wrenched her arm free from his grasp.

"Meaning me," he said hoarsely.

Bree could still feel the sensation of Will's fingers in her flesh, and she rubbed her arm.

Will looked only the slightest bit contrite. "Sorry. Don't usually go in for roughing up a gal. Then again" —a sly grin crept across those seductive lips—"don't usually have call to."

"I'm sorry if I insulted your ranch, Mr. Sheridan, and bruised your feelings. But really, I never thought real cowboys were sensitive types."

Will's free hand boldly brushed her wild cinnamon hair away from her face. "I reckon you don't know the first thing about what a real cowboy is, Bree Winston."

His hand was as tender now as it had been rough a moment before. Bree's mouth went dry, and she could feel her heart thumping against her chest. Nervously, she pulled away.

"Don't do that again," she said in a low, husky tone that unfortunately lacked the conviction she meant to convey.

Will leaned toward her. For a moment he completely disregarded what she realized had sounded more like a plea than a command. But then she saw he was merely reaching for the front-door handle. Before he swung the door open, however, his lips brushed her ear, and he whispered, "Those sound like fightin' words, ma'am. Better learn that real cowboys never flinch from a good fight."

Bree compressed her lips tightly. So Will Sheridan had succeeded, after all, in getting her completely riled before her introduction to the rest of the Sheridan Wild West Show troupe. When he opened the door, her eyes were glinting fire, and her cheeks bore a highly colorful, rosy hue.

The scene before Bree's fiery eyes was homey. Logs burned in the enormous fieldstone fireplace of the large wood-walled room, whose wide pine floors were covered with several faded but colorful hooked rugs of Northwest Indian patterns. A pair of long gray wool couches and several chairs and hassocks were grouped haphazardly around the fireplace.

In what looked like an equally random grouping, six people—four men and two women—sat warming themselves by the fire. They were listening to music that was gaily blasting on an ancient-looking phonograph player that rested on an equally ancient pine credenza. One of the women, apparently in her early fifties, was crocheting contentedly. The other woman, this one considerably younger and strikingly pretty, sat curled up close to the fire, talking animatedly to a fellow who looked more a youth than a man. He, like Will, was dressed in typical cowboy fashion: jeans, plaid shirt, and leather vest. Two men sat across from each other playing cards, using one of the hassocks as a makeshift table. The fourth man, a weathered-looking elderly gentleman with deeply etched lines in his leathery face, sat off to the side. His rawhide jaw worked away at a wad of chewing tobacco as he stared silently into the fire and slowly tipped his rocking chair back, holding it in place for an extra moment before letting it tilt forward.

Everyone but the old man stopped what they were doing and turned toward the two people standing at the closed door.

Will broke the expectant silence. "Well, folks, meet Ms. Bree Winston, the new owner of the Sheridan Wild West Show. An eastern lady who, I'd better tell you here and now, has a lot of ideas."

Bree shot him a cool look, then turned to the group, all of whom—except for the old fellow, who still hadn't glanced up—wore bemused expressions on their faces.

Bree smiled nervously. "I'm more than willing to hold off on sharing my ideas until I've had a chance to catch my breath. The ride out here," she swallowed, "plumb wore me out."

The middle-aged woman set down her crochet work on the couch. She smiled at Bree. It was the only smile the new owner got. "Well, of course, you're weary." Her lips pursed for a moment as she cast a knowing glance at Will. "And I bet you're hungry, too."

"Starved," Bree admitted, feeling the dizzying after-effects of the Scotch she'd had to drink a little while ago. As she watched the woman head off across the room to a roughly set-up kitchen area, she quickly said, "Please, don't go to any trouble. I can make myself something to eat."

The stocky woman merely shrugged. "There's only leftovers of stew from dinner, if that's all right. We eat early here, usually at five. Leaves us time to digest our meal before evening rehearsal. We'll be clearing out in a few minutes to go down to the barn to work on our routines." She was already at the old-fashioned cast-iron stove; it looked as if it had a solid slice of history about it.

"Why don't you skip rehearsal tonight, Will, and entertain the lady while she has her supper," the woman at the stove said firmly as she stirred the stew in the blue enamel kettle.

"I'm afraid Ms. Winston doesn't find me all that entertaining, Annie."

Annie continued stirring the stew, paying him no mind. "And introduce her around. This bunch here has the manners of coyotes." She gave the silent group a sweeping glance. "Well, speak up! Tell Mrs. Winston your names. Will here looks kind of tongue-tied himself." Which, of course, he didn't, Bree observed, but nor did he seem to mind Annie's badgering style in the least. In fact, he seemed to be enjoying himself thoroughly.

"Now, where's my manners gone," Annie said before any of the others could say a word. "Should introduce myself, first off. I'm Annie Taggart, born and bred here in Ritter Creek. So if you want to know anything at all about the place, you ask me."

37

Bree smiled. "Nice to meet you, Annie. And please call me Bree." She glanced awkwardly around the room, avoiding only Will. "All of you—please."

She was met with dull-eyed stares. No one else volunteered a name. It was Will who finally did the introductions.

"The two boys playing cards are Duke Forrester"— a thin-faced man with deep-set eyes glanced up and nodded, wedging his thumbs under the straps of his suspenders—"and Owen Blackstone, otherwise known as Chief Blackfoot." Dark-skinned, broad-faced Chief Blackfoot gave a quick smile and then began mindlessly shuffling the deck of cards.

"The youngsters by the fire are Joey Ross and Maggie McPhee."

The raven-haired Maggie clearly did not like Will referring to her as a youngster. And from where Bree was standing, Maggie's voluptuous curves were anything but girlish, even if she was a good five or six years younger than twenty-nine-year-old Bree.

Joey rose with easy grace from his position on the rug near the hearth and walked over to Bree. He offered his hand and a shy smile. "Pleasure to meet you, ma'am."

Bree knew Will was grinning without having to confirm it with a look. She threw back her shoulders. "It's nice to meet you, Joey. And the name's Bree."

"Yes ma'—siree. Bree," Joey said with a good-natured laugh. "I sometimes get so used to playing old-

38

time showman, I forget to drop it when the show's over."

"The show's never over," the dark-haired Maggie piped in. "You know that's Will's motto, Joey."

Bree cast a glance over her shoulder at Will. "Is that right?" she said slowly, more as a rumination than a question.

Maggie stood up and tightened the leather belt of her jeans. The tug accentuated the young woman's very narrow waist. "We're supposed to be livin', breathin' examples of a time gone by. A time when women were women"—she sashayed over toward Will —"and men were men," she finished in a sultry fashion. "Isn't that right, cowboy?"

Will smiled wryly, and he affectionately patted Maggie's behind, which was sharply defined by her tight jeans. "That's right, Calamity."

"Calamity?" Bree's brows arched.

Maggie smiled up at Will and then glanced over at Bree, not wasting the smile on her. "Didn't you ever hear of the famous lady sharpshooter of yesteryear, Bree? Why, she's a legend." Maggie sighed. "Will was right. You really are green, aren't you?"

"I've heard of Calamity Jane," Bree said icily. "I just wasn't aware you were filling her boots."

"I'm Will's . . . sidekick," Maggie answered coyly, long lashes fluttering. "A modern-day Calamity Jane," she added throatily.

The girl had a flair for the dramatic. Bree had to hand her that much.

Annie broke up the budding shooting match between Maggie and Bree by announcing that Bree's stew was ready and recess was over for the others.

"Let's hit the dusty trail down to the barn, folks," Annie ordered, snapping her palms together.

Everyone stood up except for the old gentleman, who'd been oddly removed from the discussion. Bree wondered if he was a relative of the stationmaster over at Green River.

The group shuffled out; Annie was last in line. She stopped at the door. "You comin', Grady?"

The old man didn't hesitate as much as contemplate the question. "Well . . . suppose." He rose from the rocking chair in a far more spry fashion than Bree would have guessed possible. The old man had to be close to seventy, if not over.

He walked toward the door. Will had moved to a long, low table against one wall of the main room. "Hey, Grady! You forgetting this?"

Bree gasped as she watched Will toss a huge silver-handled dagger in Grady's direction. The blade spun. To Bree's astonishment, the old man did an incredible spin and leap in the air and then caught the blade by the handle.

Both men chuckled as Bree expelled her breath. "Why, that's fantastic."

Grady opened the door, seemingly unaware of the compliment. But as he started to shut it, he suddenly paused and cast Bree a surprisingly seductive grin. "You ain't seen nothin' yet, ma'am."

When the door closed, Bree simply stood staring in amazement.

"The old geezer's still pretty good," Will said casually. "Come on and eat your stew. It's Annie's finest, and it'd be a pity to let it get cold."

Bree turned slowly to face him. "Pretty good! The man's remarkable."

"You should have seen him in the old days." Will led her over to a chair close by the fire. Annie had put a large bowl of stew on a table just beside it.

Bree sat down, and Will took a seat a few feet across from her.

"Are they all that good?" Bree asked.

Will gave her one of his cocky grins. "We all have our good points and our bad."

Bree took a bite of the savory stew. "Mm," she murmured. "Well, one of Annie's good points is definitely her stew. Why aren't you eating?"

"I ate before I went to fetch you." He gave a low laugh. "Wasn't sure I'd have much of an appetite afterward." The laugh deepened; his blue eyes trailed down her body and back up to her face. "Now I'm finding I've got . . . an appetite . . . after all."

Bree gave him an angry look. "I'll tell you one of your bad points, Mr. Sheridan. You lack finesse. You're utterly crass. And if you think I've come out here to get lassoed by some two-bit phony cowboy like you, you're sadly mistaken. I'm here for one reason only, Mr. Sheridan. Business."

"You've made that point already, Ms. Winston," Will told her.

Bree crossed her arms in front of her chest. "Well, I hope so. I suppose I've gone and bruised that sensitive ego of yours again, but I happen to believe in being honest. And the truth is, you simply don't make it in my book as a cowboy Casanova."

She paused, then took another spoonful of stew. She had difficulty swallowing it because of Will's silent, intense stare, but when she did, she said, "Now, I'm sure your sidekick would be tickled pink by your technique, Mr. Sheridan." Bree's tone was arch. "You ought to save it for her. Or have you already done that? Perhaps she's no longer new and exciting." Bree started to take another spoonful of stew, only to discover that her stomach was churning and she'd suddenly lost her appetite. "Or did you decide it might be to your advantage, Mr. Sheridan, to make a grandstand play for the new boss lady? Perhaps you thought you would keep me so occupied that I'd butt my nose out of the business side of things." She was getting thoroughly heated up now, not sure what had sparked her own angry tirade. "Well, let me tell you something, Will Sheridan—"

But before she could finish, Will sprang from his chair. He gave her an angry look, then gripped her shoulders, lifted her to her feet, and pulled her close to him. "Let me tell you something, Bree Winston. Talk about phonies—well, you take the cake. You are as phony as they come, sweetheart. If I know one thing, I

42

know when a woman's appetites are sparked. And like it or not, Bree, I spark yours—and you can't deny it."

Bree's aquamarine eyes turned stormy. "Why, you insufferable—"

Will cut her off, pulling her closer to him. "So if we're gonna talk about honesty, ma'am—" This time he cut himself off, crushing his lips down on hers, drowning out her outraged cry. When her hands pounded on his chest, he gripped them tightly, drawing them behind her back, enslaving her in his arms.

Bree struggled against the onslaught of his harsh lips. But much to her dismay, she felt her entire body respond to his fierce assault. His tongue now demanded entry into the warm recess of her mouth. She was finding it hard to breathe. Her head was swimming.

Will's head was swimming, too. What had begun as a chance to prove a point had turned into more passion than he was prepared for. Oh, he knew Bree Winston was desirable. Even as she stood on the station, disheveled, weary, a line of frustration marring her smooth brow, he'd been taken by her looks. But beautiful or not, he didn't like her type. She was snooty, headstrong, stubborn. . . .

Heat edged its way up his throat as he deepened the kiss; his tongue thrust between her teeth, arrogant and demanding. His hands stroked down her back as he pressed her hungrily against him. This is crazy, he told himself, all the while grasping her tighter, feeling the trembling muscles of her body against his as she gave up her futile struggle.

Fury and desire warred inside Bree as she gave herself up to Will's searing kiss. She wasn't sure which enraged her more—his assault on her body and senses, or her own passionate response.

Will was merciless as he continued to devour her now-pliant mouth. And as much as she fought to hide her response, Bree found herself bereft of reason. Her knees grew weak under the heady ardor of his lips, and she felt powerless to fight off the hot stabs of excitement coursing through her body. Her fingers gave up their hold on his shirt and wound themselves in his thick, dark hair, her tongue meeting his.

When at last he released her, they were both shaken. Will handled it by drawing away stiffly. His rugged features were tight; his blue eyes were darkly enigmatic.

But although Bree had to brace herself against the table for support, her blue-green eyes shone with fury —fury still mixed with desire, Will saw. Color stained her cheeks, and she tossed her head back angrily, glaring at him.

"I warned you, Mr. Sheridan." She gritted her teeth, desperate to suffocate the fire within her. Her voice was husky; that wild pulse continued to throb in the pit of her stomach. She raised her hand to strike him, but he caught her wrist in midair and held it there firmly for a moment.

"And I warned you, Bree. A cowboy worth his

weight in cowhide never backs off from a good fight."
His blue eyes warmed, the shakiness gone. Laughter
sparkled in his eyes now, catching up the corners of
his mouth. "Never."

CHAPTER THREE

"Considering the circumstances," Bree said stiffly, "and the fact that this ranch doesn't belong to me after all, I don't think I ought to stay here."

"I wasn't planning on it," Will countered sardonically. "Wouldn't want folks talking." He tilted his head jauntily to one side. "I have to preserve my reputation as an honorable cowboy for all the little tykes in town who think of Will Sheridan as a legend in his own time."

"Will Sheridan, you are so full of yourself, it's a wonder you manage to take in a breath of air," Bree drawled, realizing with dismay that she was beginning to talk as if she were in a rerun of *Death Valley Days*.

Will must have realized it too, because he was grinning broadly. His compelling blue eyes sent an entirely involuntary flash of arousal down her spine. Avoiding his amused, seductive gaze, she looked over at the suitcase still standing at the door. "If you didn't mean for me to stay here, why did you carry in my suitcase?"

Will let his eyes drop to her dusty, wrinkled suit. "I

thought you might want to change into something more comfortable."

"I'd just as soon get settled first," Bree muttered. She felt even more disheveled now, thanks to Will's unsettling kiss. She had a strong urge to tuck her shirt fully back into the waistband of her skirt to regain a semblance of order. But she fought the urge, knowing that it would only bring another insufferably amused smile to Will's lips. "Is there a motel of some sort in Ritter Creek?" She was pretty sure of the answer before Will shook his head.

"A rooming house, then?"

"Ritter Creek isn't exactly on the tourist route."

Bree compressed her lips. As she met Will's gaze, she saw that he was enjoying her predicament immensely. Her distress immediately shifted to anger. "I don't like you, Will Sheridan. I don't like you one little bit."

Will laughed, but this time it rang with a good-natured lilt. "You'd better be careful, Bree, or I might have to prove you a liar again." His smile softened as he saw her hastily take a step back. "Can't say I'd mind it. Can't really say that you would, either," he added in a teasingly insinuating tone.

Bree sighed wearily. "I don't know why you refuse to let up, Will Sheridan. Surely you know that I find your seductive manner highly insulting." She avoided considering that she also found it infuriatingly seductive. She eyed him warily. "Is that the point of all this? Do you want to humiliate me enough that I go scurrying back east on the next damned stagecoach?" She took in a steadying breath. Her temper had never felt as out of control as it had since she'd encountered this blue-eyed, fast-working cowboy. Again she steered clear of the fact that it wasn't only her temper that was rapidly getting out of control. Despite her best efforts, the sensation of Will's searing lips crushing hers continued to haunt her. She still couldn't believe how quickly and easily he'd turned her rage to desire.

Will Sheridan found himself staring at Bree's beautiful, sensual mouth—a very kissable mouth, indeed. His lips still burned with the memory of her enticing responsiveness to the one kiss they'd already shared. "Now, most women wouldn't have interpreted my attraction to them as meaning I wanted to run 'em out of town." He smiled at her, a slow, deliberate smile, as he smoothed his ruffled hair; his strong fingers raked through the thick, dark strands.

Bree had to pull her eyes away as she found herself wanting to help him with the task. Tossing her own hair back with a regal gesture, she announced, "Well, I am not most women."

Will laughed. "No. No, I suppose you're right there. Not too many women would pack their gear, turn their back on their home, their friends, their roots, and blindly head out to the wild frontier to try their hand at turning a no-account bunch of cowpokes into some kind of big-time spectacle. You've got a wild, reckless spirit in you, Bree."

She eyed him warily, unsure if he was paying her

"spirit" a compliment or having more fun at her expense. Will wore a poker face, however, and there was no way she could tell for sure. She decided she'd better trust her suspicions.

Placing her hands firmly on her hips, she said defiantly, "Whatever you think about me, Will Sheridan, is beside the point. The only thing you need to know about me is that I have no intention of returning east. Absolutely none. I've burned my bridges behind me, and I'm glad of it. I mean to stay here, Will. And I mean to accomplish everything I set out to accomplish. So if that doesn't suit you . . ." She let the sentence hang. The fact was, she knew she needed Will Sheridan, just as she knew that he couldn't quit the show even if he wanted to. When James gave her ownership of the Sheridan Wild West Show as his only concession in the divorce settlement, he had handed her the legal contract Will had signed a year ago. It bound him to the show for four more years.

Will must have known exactly what was running through her mind, because his face darkened. "Looks like you've got me over a barrel, ma'am." He broke into a sudden grin. " 'Less, of course, you want to break the contract. Just so you know, I won't take you to court for breach of promise," he said, his smile now clearly taunting.

Bree opened her mouth to retaliate and then shut it without saying a word. She looked up into those burning blue eyes of his. If he weren't so damned handsome, so fiercely compelling, she thought, I'd know how to handle him. She sighed; a sudden weariness overcame her. She'd known this would be hard, but she'd never counted on a tumultuous confrontation with the star of the show. She felt her eyes begin to mist, and she turned away before Will could notice. She didn't realize he already had.

In a muffled voice she said, "Really, what can you have against me at this point? You haven't even heard about my ideas, my plans. I'm willing to sell everything of value I own—use all my savings—to make this show a commercial success. Doesn't that prove to you I'm committed to this? Look, Will, I happen to be a very smart woman. A creative woman. Unfortunately, all you seem to see is a sexual conquest."

Will felt something stir in him at the defeated sound in her voice. Bree Winston reminded him of the wild stallions he felt compelled to tame. Like them, Bree had a proud, defiant spirit, an unrestrained exuberance, a fierce determination. Will's feelings now reminded him of the sadness that always came each time he succeeded in breaking a stallion's spirit, seeing the resigned surrender in the once-proud steed's dark eyes.

Oh, he knew he hadn't broken Bree's will, merely bruised it. But he had no doubt that she was far more vulnerable than she let on. Yes, he thought, with a strange mixture of emotions, I could break her . . . if it came to that. No cowboy liked to be owned by anyone, even if he brought it on himself. And being lassoed to a woman—well, now, that would really be rock bottom.

He walked over to the fire and leaned against the mantel. "You're wrong, Bree. Not that I don't find you enticing, but that's not all I notice. I reckon you're smart. And I'm sure you've got all kinds of creative ideas swimming around in that pretty little head of yours. The point is, we're perfectly happy the way things are right now."

Bree's eyes narrowed as she turned to face him, regaining her fiery spirit. " 'We'—or you, Will?"

The obstinate hardness spread over his features. "You saw the reception you got. No one here wants a fancy Park Avenue debutante coming out here with fancy ideas. We don't need them. We don't want them. Things are going fine right now. We're booked solid for the season. Okay, so there isn't much left over after expenses. Those of us that need more money take on other jobs, come winter. And there's still some cash left in the kitty for emergencies. Your ex-husband didn't pay a hell of a lot for ownership, but then again, I guess he figured he wasn't getting much of an investment. To us, though, the show is worth a lot. We may be a poor, motley group of cowpokes, but like I said, we're happy just the way things are."

The expression on Bree's face was as stubborn as Will's. "Well, it just so happens, I'm not happy with the way things are. And I find it hard to believe that the rest of your troupe wouldn't like to play in big cities to sellout crowds instead of in the backwater

51

towns you book the show into. And I'm willing to bet not one of them would squawk about making some big bucks. Not even you."

Will gave her a deprecating sneer. "You may know a lot about how to kiss a cowboy, Bree honey, but like I said before, you don't know anything about what makes a cowboy tick. You see success in terms of dollar signs. You want to buy yourself some happiness. Well, me—I don't need greenbacks to make me happy."

"I suppose living out here on this broken-down ranch, spending a few months of the year traipsing off to godforsaken little towns that barely pay for your gas, makes you happy."

Will grinned. "You're learning." He walked over to the door and picked up her suitcase, singing a cowboy tune about open spaces, clear blue skies, and riding as free as a dove along the lonesome range.

Bree gave him a contemptuous look.

"Come along, ma'am," Will drawled, casting an insolent glance over his shoulder. "Let's get you bedded down for the night before I decide to throw my reputation as a legendary good guy to the winds and bed you right here with me." The hardness had vanished from his face, and he raked his eyes boldly over her body.

Bree smirked at his leering study, but then her expression turned cautious. "Where will I be staying?"

"Over the barn. There are a few bedrooms up there. You can share with either Maggie or Annie."

"Annie," she said, so quickly that Will grinned.

"Now, it'll be a mite noisy for a couple of hours," he said as they walked out of the house, "but once the troupe quits its hootin' and hollerin', you'll hear nothing to trouble your dreams but a few screech owls and some lonesome coyotes."

"Does everyone in the company live over the barn?"

"During the months we rehearse they do. All 'cept old Grady, of course. He wouldn't be caught dead sleeping under a man-made roof unless it was pretty near a hurricane outside. Even then, he'd be more likely to crawl into a cave in the hills for the night rather than stay down here. Grady likes his solitude. Many's the day he heads up into the hills before dusk and camps out—sometimes for a day or two, sometimes for a week or more." He cast her a teasing look. "That's another thing you ought to know about cowboys. We all like our solitude. 'Course, some like it more than others. Now, I might spend some contented nights on the range by myself, but every now and then I hunger for a nice, soft, inviting"—he drawled the words, letting the sentence hang for a moment—"bed to crawl into."

Bree ignored the inference, focusing instead on the remarkable old man known as Grady. "But isn't it dangerous for a man Grady's age to go tramping off into the hills? I mean, you said there were coyotes—"

"Coyotes, bears, rattlers. I reckon every one of God's creatures is out there in those hills. Even a few mountain men, who are probably more dangerous than all those creatures put together. Who knows? There might even be a few renegade Indians up there in the hills," he drawled. "Better be careful if you stroll too far afield of the ranch, ma'am. Wouldn't want some mean old critter going after you."

Bree looked up at him as they walked outside. "And you don't worry about Grady camping out up there?"

"Wouldn't matter whether I worried or not," Will said. "Out here a man's got to do what a man's got to do."

"And a woman?" Bree arched a beautifully shaped brow. "What's a woman got to do?"

Will looked down at her, his blue eyes sparkling in the moonlight. He'd come to a stop, and Bree, having no idea in which direction he was taking her, was forced to stop as well. He set the suitcase down. Bree was excruciatingly aware that the taut fabric of his shirt teased the rippling muscles of his chest and arms. Once again, despite herself, she could feel her heart racing. Damn the man for doing this to her!

Will's gaze was like a caress. "A woman's got to believe in her man." He was only inches from her now. Bree could feel his warm breath fan her face. But he made no move to touch her, no move at all. So why did she feel that with a look alone he was practically making love to her?

A flash of alarm swept over her. What was happening to her? She'd never reacted this way to a man before—a perfect stranger, no less. She didn't even like Will Sheridan. No, that wasn't true. He baffled her.

His moods and manner shifted like the desert sands. He was right. She hadn't the slightest notion what made a cowboy tick. What disturbed her thoroughly was that she felt a strong desire to find out.

She could bear the nearness no longer. With no idea where she was going she began taking quick strides ahead. Will let her get a few yards in front of him, and the distance allowed her to feel a bit more composed. "The way I see it," she shouted back in his direction without slowing down, "a woman has to believe in herself first."

Will caught up to her with a few easy strides. His hand snaked out and grabbed her shoulder, forcing her to stop once more. "And do you believe in yourself, Bree?" He asked the question so tenderly, Bree had to fight a sudden impulse to cry.

She quickly averted her gaze. "I want to be able to —desperately," she said in a voice so low that she wasn't sure if Will had heard her.

But when his hand lightly skimmed her cheek in a gentle stroke, Bree knew he had heard. And, she thought with the strangest quiver in her heart, he understood. Yet when she dared to look up at him again, for some inexplicable reason his expression had hardened once more. This cowboy, Bree decided, was truly an enigma.

They walked the rest of the way down to the barn in silence. Both struggled with feelings neither one of them had expected or wanted.

The barn was close to a quarter-mile walk from the

ranch. When Bree first set eyes on it, she was taken aback. For one thing, the building was enormous, far larger than any barn she'd ever seen before. And unlike the dilapidated ranch, this place looked to be in tiptop shape, from the newly shingled roof to the freshly whitewashed siding.

Inside, the hootin' and hollerin' were still going on. Chief Blackfoot was over in one corner whooping and turning around in circles as he juggled four tomahawks. The sharp blades glistened ominously as they were caught in the kleig lights that filled the auditorium-size space. The old-timer, Grady, was off in a corner, blithely tossing knives at his target. In this instance the target was the cook, Annie Taggart, or more precisely her outline, marked in black paint on the large wooden wall she was strung up to. Bree gasped each time Grady tossed a silver dagger. As for Annie, she seemed remarkably blasé about the whole thing.

Bree turned to Will, who was standing next to her. "How can she stay so calm?" she asked incredulously.

"Grady rarely misses," Will said with a wink.

Bree gave him a wry smile but then immediately turned her wide-eyed attention back to the center of the arena, where there was an elaborate stage set of a typical frontier town's main street, complete with general store, pony express office, hotel, barbershop, jailhouse, saloon, and bank.

Joey Ross, the young cowboy who'd been talking to Maggie McPhee back at the ranch, was just stepping out of the saloon, or rather swaying out it. A typical cowboy who'd had a few too many for the dusty trail. A moment later the door to the jail swung open. Duke Forrester, wearing a shiny sheriff's badge and looking every bit the tough, no-nonsense lawmaker, casually stepped out and ambled next door to the pony express office. As soon as he disappeared from view, Joey's whole demeanor changed. Pulling out a red bandanna from his pocket, he tied it bandit-style around his face and whipped out a gleaming silver pistol. With a furtive glance, he headed into the bank.

Bree jumped as the sound of gunshots exploded in the cavernous barn. Will put a friendly arm around her, watching with a smile her obvious fascination as Joey came bursting back out onstage, clasping the screaming bank teller, played to the hilt by Maggie McPhee, only to run smack dab into Sheriff Duke Forrester. What ensued was a rousing shoot-'em-up, spiced with some fabulous acrobatic antics by both the bandit and the sheriff and followed by a breathtaking aerial walk along the thin ledge of rooftops by Joey and his reluctant hostage, Maggie.

Bree watched with heart-stopping awe as the two did their stunts. They finally came to the end of the roof. Sheriff Forrester made his way along the ledge after them.

"Looks like the bad guy's come to the end of his rope," Bree grinned.

"Never underestimate a bandit, ma'am," Will answered with a wink.

Sure enough, out from behind the stage set, an exquisite ebony stallion appeared, tossing its large, proud head and pawing at the hard-packed dirt of the barn floor. Just below the bandit and his hostage, the steed came to a restless halt.

Bree gasped as Joey swept Maggie up into his arms, leaped off the roof, and landed with expert precision on the leather saddle of the beast. With a whoop and a holler, the two rode off down the main street, disappearing around the set. Meanwhile, the sheriff, now teetering on the ledge, let out a scream of distress.

Without realizing it, Bree clutched Will's arm as Forrester went sailing through the air, "miraculously" landing in a huge pile of hay that just happened to be stacked up on the boardwalk in front of the general store.

"That was absolutely terrific!" Bree exclaimed. Only then did she realize she was gripping Will's strong, muscular arm. She released the hold immediately, not missing Will's smile, which was clearly amused but also oddly tender. For an instant Bree felt that quivery sensation again.

His hand brushed her cheek. The touch was as tender as the smile. Bree felt unnerved. The feeling only increased as he lowered his head; his lips were very close to her ear. "The show's not over yet," he whispered. And then, before she had a chance to retreat, he bit her earlobe playfully and then took off at a fast, graceful clip.

Bree watched, tight-lipped, as he headed across the

barn and disappeared behind the stage set. She could still feel the sensation of his nibble and cursed herself silently for the tiny shiver it sent down her spine. Thankfully, her attention was drawn away from that most disturbing feeling when she saw Joey reappear on his glistening black stallion. Maggie was still cussin' and kickin' in his arms. As Joey led the horse at a fast clip around the arena, Will reappeared, this time not on foot but on an exquisite white steed that put the Lone Ranger's Silver to shame.

As Will chased after the bank robber and his hostage, he performed an amazing series of daredevil stunts that took Bree's breath away. But that was only the beginning. In the midst of those acrobatic wonders on horseback, Will withdrew his trusty rifle, which had been secured to the saddle, and began proving why the stationmaster at the Green River depot had proclaimed Will Sheridan just about the best sharpshooter around. A series of cleverly displayed targets were arranged along the stage set. First there was a small gold knob atop the barber pole outside the barbershop. Then Annie came strolling out of the general store carrying a gaily spinning pinwheel in each hand. Grady got into the act, too. He ambled out of the saloon with a deck of cards in his hand. Every time Will made a run by, Grady held a card up in his outstretched hand. Toward the end, he was tossing them up in the air.

Will never missed a target. Bree was dazzled. She found herself clapping enthusiastically when Will turned his attention to the runaway bandit and shot off Joey's dark brown suede Stetson, sending it flying off his head into the air. Will fired again, and this time Joey pretended to be hit in the arm. Now it was his turn and Maggie's to perform a series of wonderfully choreographed stunts on the ebony stallion. Joey's final stunt was a clownish somersault off the horse onto the ground. The sheriff suddenly appeared from behind the set to nab him as he lay there eating dust.

Meanwhile, the poor, hapless heroine of the piece was screaming in alarm; she had lost the reins of the stallion and was shouting for Will to rescue her. He did, with a fabulous display of derring-do. Bree couldn't help but notice that Maggie threw herself into the part as Will swept her off her horse and into his strong arms. Maggie's whole voluptuous body clung to him; her slender arms were wrapped tightly around his neck as he slung one arm protectively around her narrow waist, taking her off on his white charger into the sunset.

Bree felt an unbidden flash of jealousy as she watched Will's "sidekick" tilt her head up and kiss her brave, wildly handsome rescuer fully on the lips. He brought his horse to a halt after a few circles around the arena. Bree told herself it was all part of the performance, but it was the most realistic-looking stage kiss she'd ever seen. Not only did her jealousy disturb her, but she caught Will opening one eye before the kiss had ended and winking at her with obvious awareness of her feeling.

Bree glowered. But by the time the rehearsal ended a couple of minutes later, she had regained her composure and rushed over to congratulate the troupe.

"Why, you're fantastic, each and every one of you!" she exclaimed to the weary-looking bunch. Their clear exhaustion did not dissipate her abundant enthusiasm. This show was better than her wildest dreams. Bree had been pretty glib when she'd told Grace that all she'd have to do was add a little glitter to the show. Secretly, she had been afraid she'd come face-to-face with a tawdry group of hapless imposters who staged a laughable show. Her ex-husband had certainly given her that impression. But James had rarely told her the truth about anything; Bree wondered if James had ever even seen the Sheridan Wild West Show. A growing excitement shot through her as she realized she truly did have a potential gold mine on her hands.

As the group began cleaning up, Bree was practically gushing. "I say, with real knockout costumes, a busload of extras to fill out the show, a few more sets, and some general sprucing up, we could hit some of the major county fairs and big-city arenas. And that's just for starters. Why, I can see us ending up in Madison Square Garden playing to a packed house." Bree waited for a sign of enthusiasm from even one member of the troupe, but she didn't get it. They were all busily tidying up, paying her no mind, eager to turn in after a hard night's work. Will seemed to be the only one listening, and his response was anything but enthusiastic.

"The farthest east we ever go is a little town north of Topeka, Kansas. Any more east than that, and the bunch of us starts wheezin' and coughin'. It must be that rarefied eastern air blowing in that does it to us."

Bree scowled as the rest of the troupe chuckled. She looked to Annie, hoping for support from the enemy camp, but Annie was having a good laugh along with the rest.

Only Grady wasn't laughing. But he had such a faraway look in his eyes that Bree couldn't imagine he'd ever take her side—or any side, for that matter. Then, just as she was having that thought, he turned and gave her a smile that held a hint of sympathy. He ambled over to her. "One thing you oughta know about Will. He always likes to get the last laugh."

Bree grinned derisively. "I've met the type before."

Will turned their way. He'd obviously overheard what they'd said. She expected him to give her one of his taunting smiles. But he didn't look at her at all. He was giving Grady his full attention. And the look the two men shared was filled for an instant with electric tension. The next instant, Grady sauntered out of the building.

Bree stared at Will, baffled. When he met her gaze finally, he gave her a careless smile. But Bree wasn't fooled. She felt certain he'd manufactured the smile for her benefit and that inside he was coiled as tight as a spring. The question was why.

Now, how was she ever going to put this cowboy out of her mind when he kept sparking her curiosity—not to mention some other disturbing emotions as well?

CHAPTER FOUR

"I haven't seen Grady around for a few days, or Will," Bree said, trying for a casual air.

Annie Taggart finished dabbing some night cream onto her face. She caught Bree's eye in the bedroom mirror. Annie smiled. "Grady's off in the hills somewhere. He'll show up again soon enough."

Bree waited, but it was clear that Annie wasn't going to make it easy for her. "And Will?" she asked finally.

Annie swiveled around to face Bree. "You sure got it bad, honey, don't you?"

Bree stiffened. "I don't know what you're talking about, Annie."

Annie chuckled good-naturedly. Over the past two weeks, Annie had gotten to know Bree Winston better than Bree knew. Annie saw right through that protective facade of hers. And unlike the rest of them in the troupe, Annie didn't get riled by what the others saw as Bree's interference. Annie knew the woman meant well. She was just confused and scared of failing.

"I can't imagine what's so amusing, Annie."

There it was, that touch of hurt in her voice, even now. Annie stopped laughing. "Don't let it trouble you, Bree. There's hardly a gal this side of the Pecos that doesn't lose her heart to Will. He does that to women."

"I'm sure he's very successful with some women." Bree swallowed. "Take Maggie, for instance." She looked away uncomfortably as she saw Annie's lips curve into a faint smile. "But I don't happen to—"

"Most women, though, are savvy to his ways and don't take him too much to heart," Annie said, cutting Bree off.

Bree got up from her bed, an irate expression on her face. "And you think I'm not savvy to his ways?" Bree laughed stridently. "Oh, I'm savvy, all right. I've known plenty of men like Will Sheridan. I guarantee you that."

Annie's smile turned tender. "No, honey. You've never met a man like Will Sheridan. Not ever in your life. He's one of a kind." Annie walked over to her bed and crawled in. "Well, tomorrow's another day," she said with a philosophic yawn. As she leaned over to switch off the lamp on the bedstand between the two single beds, she continued idly, "And Will will more than likely be getting back from up north tomorrow with a couple more horses"—she grinned—"and I hope with some little gal to take my place as Grady's assistant in his knife-throwing routine. Problem is, every time Will brings a pretty young thing over to meet

Grady, she takes one look at the old guy and starts shakin' in her cowgirl boots. And Grady, that old devil, he starts playin' up to her fears for all they're worth, his hands trembling, his eyes squinting, acting clear loco around her. That old man is set in his ways, all right. Doesn't take to change too well at all. It never fails—you give him a few minutes with one of them gals, and she's racing off faster than a she-cat. Not even Will's sweet talk can win her over then. But I warned Grady I was going to quit after this season, come hell or high water. So he'd better start training a new gal if Will brings one down."

Bree lay back in bed and stretched out. It was an unusually warm night, and she didn't bother with any covers. "I didn't think you minded being Grady's assistant. You seem so calm about it. Why, you hardly blink when those knives start flying."

"Oh, I'm not nervous about Grady. I'd trust that old geezer with my life." She chuckled. "Guess I already proved that." She sighed. "It's just . . . I'm gettin' too old for this sort of thing. It's not dignified for an old lady like me to be prancin' about in a young gal's cowgirl costume, posing like some pinup queen. Now, a few years back, when I still had my girlish figure"—she chuckled—"can't say as it was too bad. No, I'll just stick with the cookin', the pickin' up after this motley bunch. I don't mind that. Feels near like I've been doing that my whole life."

"How long has it been, Annie? How long have you been with Will and the others?"

"Since it all began, honey. Must be goin' on seven years now. No, eight, I think."

"Is that when you met Will? Eight years ago?"

"The day he bought this ranch here in Ritter Creek. I've worked on this place since I was seventeen, first for Tom Keegan and his family. Then when Will took it over, he kind of took me along with the rest of the fixtures. Suited me just fine, but I'll tell you one thing, honey, I sure wasn't planning on being part of any Wild West show at the time."

"How did the show get started?" Bree asked. "Had Will worked in other Wild West shows before?

"Don't rightly know."

"What about Grady? He certainly knows how to throw those knives."

"Grady's what you call a jack-of-all-trades. Done everything from cow herding to blacksmithing. Wouldn't be surprised if he didn't do some rustlin' in his day. Joey told me Grady spent some time in the hoosegow when he was a young cowpoke."

"Has Will known Grady for a long time? Those two seem to have—I don't know—a strange kind of a relationship. There seems to be some animosity between them. Although there are times when they appear honestly fond of each other."

"Never could figure what went down between those two. I guess there was a time when they knew each other years back. But the first time I saw Grady was when he joined the show about five years ago. Then, a year or so back, Grady disappeared for a time. He and

Will had some kind of a row. Well, wouldn't you know it, just before the show went on the road again last summer, who should appear from out of the blue but the old geezer himself, acting like he'd stepped out for a pack of smokes instead of having been gone for near to three months. Will was glad he was back, though. I could tell, even though he got all tight-faced when he saw Grady that first day."

Bree turned on her side to face Annie. She could just make out the older woman's outline in the pale moonlight. "Where is Will from, Annie? He doesn't talk about himself much. Or at least I can't seem to get a straight answer out of him."

Annie chuckled in the darkness. "You're not the only one, honey. You might say Will Sheridan is a kind of a mystery man. He never talks much about himself. Oh, folks around here each have their theories, but—"

Bree propped her pillows up under her head, half sitting in bed. "What theories?"

"Oh, Will having been everything from a bounty hunter up in Wyoming to a traveling salesman for vacuum cleaners in Utah. Some say he comes from California; then there's others will swear he was born and raised down in Texas. There's one or two who even believe he comes from somewhere in the East." Annie made a clicking sound with her tongue. "I can't say as there's any more truth to that tale than any of the others, but I know one thing for sure, he's never had anything good to say about the East. And he's sure never been out that way since I've known him."

Bree's brow creased. "Maybe he was from the East and had some kind of unhappy experience there. He certainly bristles every time I talk about bringing the show to Madison Square Garden."

"Well"—Annie sighed sleepily—"my theory is that Will Sheridan is a cowboy, pure and simple. Don't matter where he comes from nor what he's done. Never was a man more of a cowboy than Will, and let me tell you, I've known quite a few of them."

Bree smiled to herself. "You know something, Annie? I'm beginning to think you're right."

Annie laughed softly. "Still doesn't stop that curiosity of yours, though, does it?"

Bree laughed, too. "Reckon it doesn't," she drawled.

There was a moment's silence. Then Annie rolled over in bed and snuggled in under the covers. "Reckon that's because you've gone and lost your heart to that lonesome cowboy, like I said in the first place."

Bree opened her mouth, then closed it. No point in arguing, she told herself. Annie was bound and determined not to believe her. Then again, she wasn't doing all that well convincing herself, either, these days.

Bree woke up at dawn the next morning. She'd been doing that since the third day she'd arrived here. Funny that back east she could barely lift her head off the pillow before noon; out here she awoke with the sun every morning feeling fresh as a daisy.

It was the excitement, she told herself, careful to clarify it as excitement about the Wild West show in general. There was so much to attend to, so much to do. She spent every afternoon and evening watching the rehearsals and every morning making plans for expanding the show, how to jazz it up for big-city audiences. Bree was thinking large scale—not only new, flashier costumes, more extras, and several stage sets instead of the one frontier town street. Bree was also working on public relations and advertising.

Nor was she content to concentrate solely on her immediate plans for the show. She was thinking ahead to the future. After the show got enough notoriety, she could imagine contacting toy companies and clothing companies. There could be Sheridan Wild West Show action figures, a line of Sheridan cowboy clothes—the sky was the limit. It could happen; Will Sheridan definitely had the kind of star appeal to make it happen. But he was also stubborn enough to make sure none of her plans got off the ground. His contract said he had to headline the show; he could do that and remain completely unruly.

Bree dressed quickly in jeans and a flannel shirt to temper the feel of the morning chill and went down to the small kitchen at the other end of the barn. She poured herself a large bowl of granola, drenched it in milk fresh from a local Ritter Creek farm, and walked down with the cereal to her favorite morning eating

70

spot by the brook behind the barn. She was sitting and eating, delighting in the feel of the crisp, fresh air against her hair and face, when she heard footsteps. She looked up to see Will approaching.

He smiled slowly as he saw the soft, rosy hue rise in Bree's cheeks.

Her heart was racing, but she forced herself to go on eating her cereal. Between munches she said as nonchalantly as she could, "Wasn't expecting you back till later in the day."

Will grinned. "Missed me, did you?"

"Can't say as I did," she drawled. "Though it has been a tad quieter around here without your daily target practice." She found herself smiling back at him; his grin was infectious.

Will made himself comfortable beside her on the log; he stretched his long, muscular legs out in front of him. Bree tried to edge away as his thigh brushed hers, but she was just about at the end of the log as it was.

"That's too much breakfast for one little gal." He snatched the spoon from her hand and helped himself to a large bite.

"Hey!" she said. "I've got a big appetite. Must be this western air."

His crooked smile accentuated the subtle dimple in his right cheek. "Must be. But I like a woman with a big appetite."

"May I have my spoon back, please?" she said evenly.

Will paid her no mind; he took another spoonful of

granola from the bowl. "Here, open your mouth if you want some. I'm willing to share."

She wrenched the spoon from his hand. The contents splattered her shirt. "Now look what you've done!" she snapped, lurching back as Will's hand moved to wipe off some strategically placed bits of cereal.

A second later, having moved a few inches too many to the left, she found herself on the hard ground with the entire bowl of cereal dumped in her lap.

Bree sat seething, but at the same time tears started rolling down her cheek. "Oh, go ahead and laugh, Will Sheridan!" she said with hot frustration. She met his gaze and saw that he was having a hard time fighting back a grin.

Will's expression turned contrite. "Come on, Bree. Why don't you loosen up a little?" He bent down over her and offered a hand. When she refused, he took the bowl away. Then he untied the bandanna around his neck, walked over to the brook, and wet the cloth.

"Here. I won't even offer to help," he said softly.

She snatched the bandanna from his hand, stood up, and wiped herself off. Head bowed, she muttered, "I wouldn't mind your help, Will, but not the kind you're willing to offer."

He tilted her chin up; his thumb lightly caressed the contour of her lower lip. "And what kind of help do you want?"

"You know perfectly well," she answered weakly. Her legs felt as if they were melting as his fingers traced her jaw. Ever since that kiss the first day they'd met, she'd been careful to steer clear of temptation. Thankfully, Will had been busy most of the time, and then he'd been gone for the past three days. But his absence seemed to have lowered her resistance.

Will felt her jaw stiffen. He lifted her head a bit higher. He could see the sun glinting in her beautiful aquamarine eyes. He could feel the heat in him rising. Slowly he lowered his face.

Just as his lips reached hers, Bree turned her head sharply to the right. His lips brushed her cheek. "Bree . . . what if we helped each other a little?" he whispered softly; his arms moved around her waist.

She struggled out of his grasp and turned away from him. He didn't fight her, but he didn't retreat. She could feel his warm breath against the back of her hair.

"Why keep pulling away from something you want, Bree?"

Bree's whole body tensed. "It isn't what I want." But even to her own ears, her voice sounded lame.

His hands lightly stroked her shoulders. She wanted to pull away, but somehow she felt frozen, rooted to the spot.

"You're as tight as sprung steel," he murmured. His touch became more of a seductive massage, first along her shoulders, then down her spine.

He lifted her thick cinnamon hair that glinted with gold in the sun. His fingers pressed gently but firmly along her neck, forcing an unbidden sigh from Bree.

Slowly, deliberately, he lowered his head again; this time he let his lips caress the softly scented curve from just below her earlobe down to her shoulder. He could feel her tremble.

When he turned her around to face him, her eyes were moist. "Why are you doing this to me?" she whispered huskily.

"Because I want to."

Her eyes narrowed. "And you think that's reason enough?"

He shook his head slowly, his smile tender and seductive. "And because you want me to."

He studied her face for a moment. It had become a luscious honey hue since she'd arrived two weeks before. He thought she had never looked more desirable than she did at that moment, nor had he ever been more struck by her rare beauty.

Who actually made the first move was impossible to judge. One minute they were staring into each other's eyes; the next, they were in each other's arms, their lips meeting in simultaneous passion. Bree's lips parted; the hunger she'd been fighting from the first burned her. Her arms moved around his neck, and her fingers twined in his thick, dark hair.

"Bree," Will murmured huskily as his lips roamed eagerly across her face. His thumbs tenderly stroked her beautifully etched cheekbones. Tremors raced through him as she pressed her body more tightly to him; a ragged sigh escaped her lips as he sought her mouth once more.

The sound of leaves being crunched underfoot caused Bree to pull away from him.

"Someone's coming," she said, still breathless from his kisses and from the passion consuming her.

"Probably a doe or a coon." Will smiled.

He went to draw her back into his arms, but Bree's hands pressed against his chest. "Will, no!" She fought for control. "How would it look if someone from the troupe came by and saw us?"

Will's smile broadened. "Reckon if it was one of the boys, he'd be right filled with envy. And if it were Annie, she'd have herself a good chuckle."

Bree arched a brow. "And if it were Maggie McPhee?"

Will cupped her chin; the tip of his index finger traced the outline of her lip. "Is that a spark of jealousy I see in those glittering blue-green eyes of yours?"

Bree hesitated. "Leave Maggie aside for the moment. We hardly know each other, Will. And the relationship that we do have is rather . . . complicated." She smiled dryly. "For one thing, it was forced upon you. You've certainly made it clear how you feel about my owning the show."

"Your owning the show doesn't trouble me as much as your plans for it."

Bree sighed. "We've been through that already, Will." She eyed him speculatively. "You haven't answered my question about Miss McPhee."

Will looked down at her; his blue eyes were dancing

with amusement. "Now, what question was that, ma'am?"

"You know exactly what question," Bree said, shoving him hard against his chest. Will, taken by surprise, tripped over the tree stump and went careening backward. He landed with a most ungraceful thud on the hard ground. Then he looked up at Bree with an expression more of astonishment than anything else.

Bree bit back her laughter for no more than two seconds, then burst into giggles.

Will's eyes narrowed. "Oh, you think that's funny, do you?" he asked in a low, threatening voice.

"Well, it does make us kind of even. For the cereal," she managed between giggles. She extended her hand. "Come on, let me help you up."

For a moment he just sat looking at her. Then he grabbed her hand. In only a fraction of a second Bree realized his intention, but that was already too late. The next thing she knew she was falling—right on top of Will.

"That's not fair!" she gasped, struggling as his arms tightened around her.

He rolled her over onto her back and swung himself smoothly on top of her, pinning her flailing hands onto the ground.

"Will, stop acting like a child!" she muttered, even though she knew that childishness had passed the moment he'd moved onto her.

"Don't you know it's dangerous to laugh at a cowboy?" His voice was so husky, she could feel the words rumble in his chest as he pressed down on her.

"Will, don't."

"Because someone might see us?"

She closed her eyes. "Because it would only complicate matters more." Slowly she raised her lids and met his burning gaze. "And because I don't want to be just another notch on your gunbelt. Annie says—"

Will's eyes narrowed. "What does Annie say?"

Bree's lips compressed. Will rolled off her, and she sat up stiffly. "She says," Bree went on in a low, solemn voice, "that most women know not to take you seriously." She met his gaze. "And Annie thinks maybe I'd be foolish enough to . . ." She let the sentence hang. Maybe she didn't go on because she didn't want to admit to Will that Annie was probably right about her. Bree wasn't as casual and sophisticated as she pretended to be. For more reasons than she cared to analyze, she could lose her heart to this cowboy.

When Will made no response, it confirmed Bree's belief that her assumption about him was right. She stood up, then dared a glance back down at Will. He'd made no move to rise. "I have a lot of work to do. I'd better mosey on. I'm arranging some new advertising." She backed off as she spoke; Will's steady gaze was making her nervous. "I think we ought to concentrate on smoothing out our working relationship, Will." She swallowed hard. "I don't really think it would be smart to become involved physically." She was still backing up. "It really never works, mixing business with pleasure. I think we . . ." She stopped as his mouth curved into a wide grin. "I don't know why you find this so funny." She watched him sit up and then took another wary step back, afraid he was going to get up and pursue her.

"Listen here, ma'am, I gotta warn you—"

Bree shook her head firmly. "I don't need any warnings from you, Will." She took another step—and let out a gasp as she lost her footing. The ground suddenly gave way, and the next moment she went flying backward into the cold, babbling brook. Her second gasp came from the shock of feeling the icy water penetrate her clothes. The tears that followed were caused by her feeling of complete humiliation.

Will stood on the edge of the brook. For once, he was kind enough not to laugh, although he couldn't quite mask the faint smile on his lips.

A deep flush rose in Bree's cheeks. She was crying in earnest now. Will waded into the water after her.

"Are you hurt, Bree honey?" he asked, all tenderness now.

"Yes, I'm hurt," she muttered hotly, fighting back tears but unable to keep her teeth from chattering. "My pride is hurt. And I hold you completely responsible. Ever since I met you, I've experienced more embarrassment, humiliation—"

"Whoa there, ma'am! I was the one trying to warn you—"

"Oh, shut up!" she snapped. "Just go away and

leave me alone. Haven't you had enough laughs for one morning?"

"Come on, Bree. Now who's acting like a child?"

"I am not acting like a child!" She tried to get up, but leather-soled boots made it hard for her to get a secure footing on the slippery pebbles. Before she was halfway up, she fell backward into the icy stream again. Will crossed his arms in front of his broad chest; he was watching her in open amusement now. The water came to just below the upper edge of his calf-high boots, so he wasn't feeling any particular distress.

"I'd offer to help you, ma'am, but the truth is," he drawled, "I don't trust you not to drag me in with you."

Bree glared at him as she made a second solo attempt; it, too, led to failure. "Damn it, Will!" she screamed, splashing at the water in frustration, "I hate you! I truly do!"

He smiled down at her. "All you have to do is give me your word as a lady, and I'll be happy to help you."

Bree's expression remained stubborn as she made a third stab at rising. This time she actually made it to her feet on her own, but suffered yet another crash landing when she took her first step toward the edge of the bank.

Will looked down at Bree. Even nearly drenched to the bone and looking fit to kill, the woman was a knockout. "Come on, let me help you. I'll take my chances." He made a valiant effort to control his laughter, but his lips were twitching.

"I wouldn't take help from you," she snapped, "if I had to spend the rest of my life in this damned brook."

"Bree honey, what am I going to do with you? I never did meet a gal more stubborn than you. Fact is, I never met a mule more stubborn."

"Very funny, Mr. Sheridan."

"Don't see you smiling," he teased.

Bree glowered at him; her teeth were chattering in earnest now. The brook water felt as if it were filled with ice cubes.

"Come on, Bree. It really is kinda funny if you think about it."

"Oh, sure," she snapped. "When I'm the one looking like a fool, it's funny. But when the shoe's on the other foot—"

Will let out a loud, weary sigh. "Okay, okay! Guess there's no other way to even this score," he said resolutely. Then he plunged headfirst into the chilly stream.

As Bree watched, wide-eyed, he rolled over and stretched flat out on his back in the water beside her, crossing one sodden leather cowboy boot over the other. "Well"—he turned to her, giving her a sly, seductive look—"would you say that makes us even?"

Bree stared at him in astonishment. Then she started to laugh. A moment later, Will joined in. Pretty soon they were laughing so hard, they were falling weakly against each other. Soon, without realizing how she got there, Bree found herself on Will's lap. The icy water was no longer the only cause of the shivers coursing through her body. Will's hot mouth was covering hers. Bree clung to him, fire and ice; his heated kisses melted the chill with exquisite ease.

CHAPTER FIVE

Once she'd managed, with Will's help, to get on firm ground again, Bree's reason returned, if somewhat shaken from Will's kiss.

"I'd better go and change," she muttered, trying not to look at the way Will's wet jeans accentuated his lean hips and firm, muscular thighs. Yet as she stepped back, this time careful to check her direction first, her aquamarine eyes involuntarily trailed his body, its loose-limbed grace and masculine power.

Will smoothed back his damp hair; a few wayward strands fell almost boyishly across his square brow. His blue eyes sparkled, and he made no attempt to conceal his careful inspection of her body, which was well defined by her own wet clothes. "You walk back into the barn looking like that, and you're likely to get some hearty ribbing, ma'am."

Bree's hand rose to her throat. She gave Will a wan look. "What would you suggest?"

"Come back to the ranch with me. I can dig up some dry clothes for you to throw on, and I'll start a fire to dry off your things."

Bree shook her head. "No, that won't be necessary. I'll manage."

But Will was in no state to be turned down. Without ado, he gathered her up in his arms. "Bree honey, I've had just about enough of your stubbornness for one morning. Anyway," he said in a perfectly casual tone as she squirmed furiously in his arms, "I brought back two fine-looking stallions this morning, and I want you to see them."

"Will, this is ridiculous! Put me down," she demanded as he headed east, away from the barn.

"Do you ride?" he asked, paying her no mind.

"Will, I mean it! You put me down this instant!" she said, struggling more earnestly.

Will merely tightened his grip on her. She was no match for his powerful strength. He had her roped in firmly.

This called for feminine tactics. "If you don't put me down, I'm going to start screaming bloody murder. What will that do to your reputation, Mr. Will Sheridan?"

Will's brows lifted. "What's it going to do to yours, Ms. Winston? I'd say we make quite a sight, the two of us. Wonder what the gang will make of it—the boss lady and the star of the show both soaked to the bone on this fine, sunshiny day."

"Okay, point well taken," she admitted reluctantly.

He grinned.

"You can put me down now. I'll accept your offer— of dry things," she added firmly.

83

He just kept walking.

Bree continued to protest, making weak attempts to gain her freedom. At the same time she also struggled with her own desire, which was escalating sharply as her body pressed sharply against his, and at the clean fresh scent of him, at the feeling of masculine power that exuded from his every pore.

Not until he'd carried her inside the main room of the ranch did he finally set her down. She stumbled and he caught her, but Bree struggled free of his grip this time, although she drew herself up with some difficulty.

Will was none too steady himself. For two weeks now he'd been fighting off his attraction to Bree. She might be extraordinarily desirable, but he was wary of her. There were bound to be clashes. They were worlds apart in how they saw the show, in how they saw life. Besides, Bree had breeding and education. She might be a fish out of water here, but she would feel at home in many more places than he ever would. This was home to Will—the mountains, the prairies, the little hick towns where he took the show, this ranch. He felt certain that this could never be home to Bree. He knew the type. In a few months Bree would grow weary of her new hobby, and there would be desolation, tedium. Right now it was new and exciting. He was new and exciting. But he felt certain that it would all wear thin and that Bree would be heading back east before the winter frost set in. So why was he hell-bent on pursuing her? Why couldn't he leave well enough alone? How could he fight her plan to turn his down-home western show into a three-ring circus and make love to her at the same time?

The answer was as simple as an answer can be. He couldn't help himself. He wanted Bree. He wanted her with a fire that just wouldn't stop burning. And he could see by the looks she tried hard to conceal that she had the same fiery need. But she was wary just as he was. She didn't trust him. He didn't suppose she ought to trust him any more than he trusted her. But he supposed that didn't change anything, not for either of them.

"You'd better get out of those wet things." His voice was husky. "I'm afraid you'll have to make do with one of my shirts, but in the meantime I can probably dig up a smaller pair of jeans in the shed for you. My hands on the ranch usually leave a few extra pairs there."

Bree looked around, unsure where to go. This was the only room in the ranch she'd been in, and then only that first evening. Since then, rehearsals had escalated, and the troupe had taken only quick breaks for meals down at the barn.

Will, seeing her hesitate, walked across to the second door off the main room. "This way. Bathroom's next door if you want to wash up."

Bree noticed the muscle working in his jaw. Could he be feeling as uneasy as she?

He stood at the doorway of his bedroom. She had to edge past him to enter. It was a large room, scantily furnished—the large bed in the middle of the room stood out glaringly. It was unmade, and she imagined she could still see the outline of his shape in it. The covers were all tangled at the bottom. A pair of his jeans and a worn shirt were tossed haphazardly over the brass footboard. He was a restless sleeper, she thought, her whole body tensing.

He was right behind her. Her stomach curled tightly as she felt his hand move against the flat of her back and nudge her forward.

"Relax, Bree," he said softly. "Sorry about the mess. I got in so late last night, I wasn't up to tidying the place this morning. You'll find a clean shirt in the closet. I'll go change out in the shed. Be back in about fifteen minutes."

Bree merely nodded. Just standing here in Will's bedroom with him beside her stirred threateningly intimate thoughts.

He touched her shoulder. Bree jumped.

Will cupped her chin. "You're as skittish as a newborn foal, Bree. Will fifteen minutes be enough time for you?"

Her eyes met his. "Yes, that's fine."

His mouth curved into one of his irresistible smiles. "Unless you need any help."

Bree eyed him wryly. "I'll manage on my own, cowboy."

He gave a disappointed shrug as he exited. "I'll get the fire going so you can lay your wet things out before I go out to the shed."

When the door closed, Bree expelled a tremulous breath. Then slowly she looked around the bedroom. Besides the bed with its old brass head and footboards, there was only a large worn brown armchair, a simple pine bureau, and a cluttered rolltop desk off by a window. The walls were of wood, like the outside of the ranch, and the aroma of timber coupled with Will's musky scent filled the room.

She glanced at the desk; an unbidden curiosity touched her sharply. Would she learn something about Will in those papers piled there? Shocked at herself even for considering such a thing, she walked resolutely toward the closet.

Here especially, Will's scent was strong. Idly, her fingers skimmed his things—mostly jeans and an assortment of rugged shirts, the kind that dramatically highlighted his cowboy appeal. Her mind drifted into fantasy; she imagined Will Sheridan transported back in time to those wild frontier days. She couldn't decide if he'd have been an outlaw gunslinger or a lawman. He was, she felt, a little of both. She smiled to herself, imagining him first in one role, then in the other.

A soft rap on the door startled her out of her daydream.

"Yes?" she called out nervously, quickly pulling a red-and-brown plaid shirt from a hanger and closing the closet door. The last thing she wanted was for Will to discover her mooning over his clothing. She'd suffered enough embarrassment for one day.

"Need anything before I head for the shed?"

"No," she said adamantly.

He laughed softly. "Okay. I get the message. Oh, I left a clean towel for you in the bathroom."

"If you want, you can take your shower first," Bree said, moving closer to the door.

"I'll use the outdoor one behind the shed. I prefer it, actually."

Bree stood close to the door. "Thanks, Will."

"Anytime, ma'am." His voice was low, almost a caress.

Bree smiled to herself and held Will's shirt close to her face for a moment. Then, feeling her imagination start to run wildly away again, she hastily tossed the shirt onto the bed. As soon as she heard the slam of the screen door, she stripped out of her wet things, wrapped the extra blanket at the bottom of the bed around her, and popped next door to take a quick shower.

Back in Will's room five minutes later, she put on his shirt and walked over to the bureau in search of a brush. None was visible, but there was an old tin cracker box; its lid was partially open. Spotting a hairbrush inside, Bree lifted the lid and reached in. There were a bunch of odds and ends in the tin—a couple of pens, some paper clips, and a few string ties with ornamental silver clasps. When Bree lifted up the brush, she noticed one more item, a curious one. It was a small oval etched gold locket. Bree stared at it for a moment. Lips compressed and feeling almost wanton, she delicately lifted the piece and studied it in the palm of her hand. There was a tiny catch. She hesitated and then compressed it. The locket opened to reveal a tiny photograph.

It was a miniature snapshot of a young woman—a very pretty, elegant-looking woman. The photo wasn't new, but it was impossible to tell how old it might be. Only the woman's face was visible. Her fair hair was falling softly around her shoulders in a simple, classic style. An old sweetheart? Bree wondered with a strange aching sensation. A sweetheart he didn't want to forget, since he still kept her locket as a keepsake?

"Bree? Everything okay?" Will's voice drifted through the closed door.

Taken unaware, Bree nearly let the locket drop into the tin, then realized with alarm that Will might pick up the sound. Gently but hastily she set it back where she had found it—along with the brush, forgoing her hair.

The door opened a crack. "Bree? Are you decent?"

She moved swiftly away from the bureau. "As decent as a woman can be in a man's shirt and nothing else," she said in a tone that was flippant purely from nervousness. How awful if he had discovered her snooping in his personal belongings!

Will opened the door wide; his gaze was amused and delighted. "Looks better on you than it does on me."

She smiled, suddenly shy. "What happened to the jeans?" she asked, seeing he was empty-handed.

"Sorry. Out of luck. There were only a couple of

pairs, and neither of them was exactly fit for further wearing."

"Oh," Bree said, feeling very exposed even though Will's cotton shirt came nearly down to her knees, because underneath the voluminous shirt she was stark naked.

Will gathered up her wet clothes.

"I can do that," she said, finding it too intimate to have him handling her lacy underthings.

Typical of Will, he paid her no mind. She ended up following him out to the main room, where the fire was blazing in the hearth.

Once he'd laid her things out over a chair near the fire, he turned to her. "Come and sit down. There's some coffee on the stove if you want some."

She hung back near the kitchen area. "No, thanks. I don't really like coffee."

He smiled. "Okay, then. Just come over by the fire. You still look a little chilled."

Bree hesitated.

"I don't bite."

She laughed dryly. "I seem to recall that you do."

"Come here, Bree," he said softly; his voice was too persuasive for her to refuse.

She moved tentatively across the room. As she neared, Will picked up the scent of his soap on her skin. A rush of arousal flowed through him, and he stared at her intently.

Will's compelling blue eyes held Bree mesmerized.

The air was electric with anticipation as excitement threaded through her nerves.

Only with great effort did she finally pull her eyes away. "Maybe I will have some coffee." Her voice was tremulous.

"Bree."

The sound of her name on his lips made her body quiver. He cupped her chin.

"We aren't children, Bree. We're all grown up. With grown-up needs, grown-up desires. Don't you think . . ."

She started to shake her head, but Will held her jaw firmly.

"Don't go denying it, Bree. You want me as much as I want you."

"It isn't as simple as that," she protested in a voice rendered breathless by his nearness, by the potent urgency in him.

"It is simple—and as basic as time itself."

Bree felt herself swept up into a vortex of emotion. Her eyes drifted up to his again, and she saw smoldering light reflected there. "It would be such a dumb thing to do," she practically moaned.

His mouth curved into a slow, deliberate smile. "You don't believe that."

"I do."

"Okay. It's dumb. Maybe for both of us."

"And that doesn't bother you?"

With one hand on her shoulder and the other smoothing back her wild cinnamon hair, he breathed in deeply. "I told you once," he whispered, his voice heavy with desire. "Out here a man's got to do what a man's got to do."

As he spoke, his hand tightened around the strands of her hair, and he drew her against him with a fevered grasp. Too late to struggle, Bree let out a tiny cry of pain and pleasure as his mouth descended over hers with driving pressure, claiming her lips with hunger and need that were explosive.

His rough intensity frightened her—or maybe it was her own spiraling need heading out of control.

"Please don't, Will!" she pleaded when at last he released her. "It's all happening too fast."

She was surprised at how willingly he let her go. But when he stepped back, she saw the fire still smoldering in his eyes.

She turned away. "I'm always rushing headlong into things," she said in a quiet voice. "And then, when it's too late, when I'm committed"—she stiffened—"I get hurt."

"You talking about your ex-husband?"

Bree turned around to face Will. "You sound surprised. It wasn't a marriage of convenience, if that's what you think," she said sharply. "I was in love with James. I trusted him." She sighed. "No, that's not true. I didn't trust him. I knew his reputation. I was duly warned by everyone who knew him. But I wouldn't listen. I thought it would be different for us. I suppose I believed I could change him. But he didn't change." Bree's eyes misted. "I did. I stopped believing in miracles. I finally got wise." She bit down on her lower lip and lifted her eyes to meet Will's. "And I don't want to get hurt again."

Will took hold of her hand gently. "Being hurt makes a person wary," he said tenderly. "I understand that, Bree."

She studied his solemn expression. "Do you, Will? Do you really know what it feels like for someone to betray your trust?"

He didn't say yes or no, but his eyes held the answer. There was depth there that Bree had not seen before. And then in a low-timbred voice he said, "Somewhere along the road, you've got to unload the burden of that hurt, or it will destroy you."

Bree thought about the photograph inside the locket. She felt certain that the pretty woman with the lovely, fair hair had once hurt Will—deeply. She longed to ask him about her. Who was she? What had happened between them? Why had she hurt him? But to ask him about her she would have to admit that she had been snooping.

He gently stroked her cheek. "Bree, if you're looking for assurances from me, there are no guarantees, any more than you can guarantee you won't hurt me. Nothing's ever sure, especially not in the beginning."

"We've got a lot of strikes against us." She was afraid to meet his gaze.

"Don't strike me out, Bree."

"I don't know what to do, Will. I'm confused. I'm scared."

With the palms of his hands he stroked her cheeks and drew her hair back gently. "Oh, Bree, let it happen."

She felt the tremor in his hands, and as he drew her into his arms, she could feel the rise and fall of his chest, the restlessness and hunger surging through him.

"Oh, Will!" she whispered; all subterfuge and hesitation fled like grains of sand blown by a desert wind. "I do want you—I do!"

He swept her up into his arms. This time she didn't struggle. It was Will who, for an instant, felt caution: she was so vulnerable, and there was no doubt of the power he wielded over her, a power he wasn't at all certain it was fair to wield. Yet he felt driven to it, aching to make love to Bree. It clawed at him.

Bree felt his momentary tension. Her eyes darted up to his; she felt as if she had stopped breathing.

There was such longing, such expectation in her eyes, and her warm, tawny skin glowed with excitement. "You're so beautiful," he whispered. He took her mouth hungrily while she clasped him fiercely around the neck; powerful, driving masculinity emanated from his tall, muscular body.

This was what she'd wanted almost from the first— to be held fast in his arms, to feel the urgency of his lips on hers, to slide her fingers up through his dark brown hair.

He trailed hot kisses randomly across her face as he carried her into the bedroom. With reckless abandon he fell onto the sheets with her; his hands moved over her, caressing her, arousing her with a longing from which there was no retreat.

Bree was held breathless by the speed with which he rid them both of their clothes. She gasped in exquisite pleasure as the heat of his naked body pressed into her flesh.

"Oh, Will, you're beautiful, too!" she whispered fervently as she hungrily kissed his neck. Her hands stroked down his back, then curved wantonly over his buttocks.

Will drew her head up. His eyes dancing with desire and tender amusement. "Beautiful? Don't you know that's a dangerous thing to call the roughest, toughest sharpshooting cowboy this side of the Pecos?"

Bree smiled a warm, seductive smile. "Well, cowboy, what are you going to do about it?"

With a laugh, he ruffled her damp hair, then caught hold of her lower lip and nibbled it with his teeth.

"And you said," she mumbled, "that you don't bite."

"Reckon you get me carried away, ma'am," he whispered heatedly against her parted lips. His hands stroked her, seemingly able to reach everywhere.

Bree's aquamarine eyes shimmered. "Reckon a woman's got to do what a woman's got to do," she murmured, and kissed him hard, letting her tongue caress his and feeling the thrill of possessing and being possessed.

They kissed until they were breathless and their lips

bruised. Then with slow, sensual movements he began brushing his lips and tongue over the soft, lovely contours of her body.

Bree's fingers trailed down his back in light, feathery strokes. She loved his tender exploration and thrilled to the nibbling bites, the moist warmth of his mouth.

His caresses grew more ardent; his lips captured first one sweet, taut nipple, then the other, rolling each over with his tongue with provocative leisure. Bree's senses began to reel. Her body trembled and she arched into him.

"Will, that feels so good," she murmured with such innocent, abandoned pleasure that it brought a smile to his lips as he continued his fiery exploits.

His tongue trailed across her taut, satin-smooth stomach. His hand slipped between her open thighs, and as his mouth moved to her heated pulsating core, Bree gasped at the invasion, then at the delicious warmth surging through her entire body.

She'd really had had little experience making love— only to James before now. Although their lovemaking had been satisfying at the time, Bree now realized how much she had missed. Unlike James, Will was bold, reckless, and undaunted. Will drove her to heights of breathless abandon. For the first time, she didn't hold back.

His body covered hers. Bree ran her hands feverishly over the length of him. Only his complete possession could give her the release her body craved. Her hips arched against him. "Please, Will! I want you so. I want to be yours." The admission came of its own volition. Agony and bliss collided against each other and gripped her senses until she was mindless with an all-consuming need.

Will poised above her, his eyes almost cobalt. Bree could see passion grip his powerful frame. Then, with a wild fervor, he entered her. "I want to make you mine. You are mine." The words were strangled, a blur to her dazzled senses, but she could feel the meaning. With his powerful, demanding lovemaking, he was branding her his. Whatever happened afterward, Bree knew with absolute certainty that for her that brand would be indelible.

Her mouth moved against his as he plunged into her with driving intensity. "I am yours," she murmured; her body met each powerful thrust, welcoming him, seeking him.

Together they cried out with the wild abandon that had consumed their entire lovemaking. Violent shudders exploded within them, intermingling and releasing for each an exquisite flood of ecstasy.

Yes, Bree thought afterward as they lay still entwined together. Branded.

Will looked down at her and watched with delight as a warm smile curved on Bree's lips, lighting up further her beautifully radiant face. She met his gaze. He smiled down at her, a smile of possession.

"That was quite a beginning, cowboy," Bree whispered, desire still apparent in her eyes.

He tilted her head up and once again tasted the sweetness of her lips. "The show's not over yet, ma'am," he whispered back seductively, drawing her more tightly in his arms.

Bree closed her eyes. She knew then that she wanted the show never to end.

CHAPTER SIX

The landscape was still strange and new for Bree, but it was becoming more familiar. It seemed impossible that she'd only been in Ritter Creek for three weeks— three glorious weeks. Bree had never felt so happy.

Soft, cool breezes whispered through the blue spruce and aspens as Bree and Will rode their black stallions through the hills. The smell of dew was fresh on the grass; a sliver of yesterday's moon still hung in the misty blue sky.

Bree spurred her steed on, digging her heels lightly into his hide. As she pulled past Will, she glanced back at him and gave him a challenging smile. Her cinnamon hair billowed about her shoulders and its wild strands fluttered in the wind as she broke into a canter.

Will grinned. There was pride in his eyes. Bree sat a horse well. These morning rides with her had become a highlight of his day. Not, of course, the only one; being with Bree brought many highlights, he was fast discovering. His grin settled into a contented smile as he watched her take off, giving her the privilege of a brief lead.

By the time he caught up to her, Bree had dismounted and was picking columbines and wild asters by the side of the trail. He swung gracefully off his horse and settled down onto the ground beneath a cottonwood tree. Bree came over with her bouquet and plucked out a lustrous pink aster. She kneeled beside Will and stuck the flower into the band of his cowboy hat.

Will drew her down onto his lap. "What kind of desperado wears a flower in his Stetson?" he challenged in a teasing tone.

"Is that what you are, a desperado?" Her tone was bantering, but her eyes searched his with serious intent.

Will laughed softly and stroked her cheek. "I did steal your heart, didn't I?"

She laid her head against his chest. "Yes," she whispered. "You stole it completely."

He let his fingers run through her wild hair, a pleasure to which he'd grown joyously accustomed.

Bree sighed. "It's all going so well, isn't it?" She lifted her head to meet his gaze. "I mean—us, the rehearsals. Everyone's in such good spirits." She hesitated. "Except Grady, maybe. He seems so removed from everything most of the time. Then every so often he'll be real friendly"—she grinned—"even a touch flirtatious. Not just with me—all the women, especially Annie. I wouldn't be surprised if that old man had a soft spot in his heart for that lady. But he certainly gives little away. I just can't figure him out, no matter how hard I try."

"Don't try," Will said casually, but Bree picked up an edge in his voice.

"Don't you like Grady, Will?"

"Isn't a question of like."

She could see his features draw into hard planes. Talking to Will about Grady was touchy. Talking to him about anything to do with his past was, too. But Bree was growing weary of sidestepping issues that were becoming increasingly important. She was falling in love with Will Sheridan, and yet she still knew nothing about him. She could only surmise that his life had left little room for trust.

Bree knew Will's response was intended to end the discussion, but she persisted. "What are your feelings toward Grady?"

"Grady's all right. You just have to get to know him."

"And how do you do that? When he's not rehearsing, he generally vanishes into the night."

"I told you, he likes to camp up here in the hills."

Bree was silent for a minute. "Annie says you and Grady go back a long way."

Will's face was expressionless. "Does she?"

Bree eyed him intently. "When did you meet Grady? How did you meet him?"

"Don't see why that matters to you."

"Why it matters to me? Damn it, Will! Of course it

101

matters! I want to know who you are, where you came from. I want to know about—about what goes on in your mind." She hesitated. "I . . . care about you, Will." Only pride kept her from calling it love. She wanted to hear that word from Will's lips first. But she had the feeling he was waiting for her to do the same thing. It was a crazy Mexican standoff; one of many with Will Sheridan, Bree sensed. That realization didn't please her, but it didn't stop her from loving him, either.

A smile touched the corners of Will's lips. "Reckon those are sweet words to a lonesome cowboy's ears."

Bree laughed softly. "You do adore fantasy, don't you, Will Sheridan?"

"What fantasy is that?"

"The fantasy of the proud cowboy bred to the range. I remember what Maggie said that first day." Maggie now no longer felt like a threat to Bree; she believed that Maggie was suffering from a decidedly one-sided infatuation; at least, one-sided since she and Will had gotten close. Will treated Maggie with great respect and it was clear that he was proud of her talents, but he never gave her any cause to think he had more feelings for her than that.

"And what was it Maggie said?" Will asked.

"She said that you expect the whole troupe—yourself included—to live out your parts to the hilt. I'm not sure about the others, but you have no trouble with your role either on or off the stage."

"I'm not playacting, Bree," Will said; his voice wavered between amusement and annoyance.

Bree let out a sigh of frustration. "I want to know the real you. I want to know about the people in your life." *Especially the fair-haired woman whose picture was in that locket.* Ever since Bree had first set eyes on it, she'd been unable to put the woman out of her mind. She haunted Bree's thoughts.

"You know all the people in my life—the ones who count," Will said with a note of exasperation in his voice. "They're all here on the ranch—Annie, Duke, Joey, Blackfoot, Maggie, and Grady." He touched her cheek. "You," he added softly.

"We're the people in your life now," Bree retorted, an obstinate glint in her eyes. "But there had to be others before. What about when you were growing up? When you were a young man? Where were you born? What were your folks like? Do you have any sisters or brothers?"

Will was silent for a moment. "I'm not right sure where I was born."

"You never asked?"

"My mother wasn't the type you asked questions of." There was tightness in his voice.

"And your dad?" Bree asked softly.

A shield dropped over Will's features. He stood abruptly. "There was no dad to ask," he said grimly. "Come on. The horses are growing restless. They need some exercise."

Bree grabbed his hand, stopping him. "Where'd you

and your mom live when you were growing up?" she went on doggedly; something was driving her to break through the barrier Will had set up.

Will stood ramrod-still. "Lots of places. My mother never did believe in staying one place too long. As for the names of the towns—they don't matter." He looked out toward the reddish haze outlining the Rocky Mountains. "My past doesn't matter. Let's just say it was of no consequence and leave it at that."

But Bree was not about to leave it at that. She stood up with a defiant look in her eyes. "Was your past so miserable? Or"—her eyes narrowed—"was it mundane enough that it would ruin your image as a cowboy hero—for all those 'little tikes,' as you call them?"

"Bree"—his voice lowered ominously—"leave it be."

She knew she was pushing hard, but that only gave her the courage to go on to the question burning in her mind. "What about that woman whose locket you keep in your bedroom? Was she of no consequence?"

Bree saw a flicker of rage in Will's eyes. He was a man who kept a tight rein on his emotions, but he was visibly fighting for control. Bree figured the tight rein fit his cowboy credo: A man's got to do what a man's got to do. Feelings just got in a man's way. As long as Will closed himself off from her, as long as she didn't understand what had made him the man he became, it would always stand between them. Bree wanted nothing to stand between her and Will, but seeing the anger in his face, sensing the explosive rage and the an-

104

guish beneath the surface, she suddenly felt a sharp flash of fear. Maybe, she had pushed him to the edge.

However, Bree didn't give Will enough credit. As swiftly as the rage lit his eyes, it vanished. A taunting smile curved his lips. "That locket's just a trinket, ma'am." He squeezed her nose. "That's for putting that pretty little nose where it doesn't belong. You go snooping around again, and I'll take you over my knee." He was still smiling, but Bree wasn't fooled. There was no doubt in her mind that he was exerting every ounce of his will to let the subject ride. But Bree couldn't let it ride, not now that she'd admitted having seen the locket.

Will strode over to where his horse was grazing, mounted with casual grace, and headed on up the hill.

A minute later, Bree guided her steed beside his. "She was very pretty."

"Yep."

"Were you in love with her once?"

Will remained in profile. "You could say we had our ups and downs."

"What was her name?"

Will glanced across at her. "You don't give up easily, do you?"

She grinned. "You just finding that out?"

He laughed softly. "Guess I figured that from the start."

"So what was her name?"

Will dug his heels into his horse and pulled forward. Either he hadn't heard her question or—more likely—

he chose not to respond. As he quickened his horse's pace, Bree did her best to keep up with him. But she was breathless, her hair wildly tossled, as her horse crested the hill. Will had reined his horse to a stop. Bree followed suit and watched Will as he stared ahead into the distance with a faraway look in his eyes. He reminded her then of Grady. Maybe all cowboys got that look in their eyes from time to time. It was a lonely look and yet oddly content. Men like Will and Grady seemed not to mind loneliness.

"Beautiful country," he said in a low-timbred voice.

Bree looked over the hillside; the earthy tones of the land no longer looked somber to her. The morning mist was rising; the outline of the mountain ridges was sharpening; the vista was majestic. "Beautiful," she agreed enthusiastically.

Will dismounted and sat down on the grassy knoll. With quiet casualness, he lifted his tobacco pouch from his shirt pocket and rolled himself a smoke. Tipping his hat up slightly, he leaned his elbows into the ground and gazed up at the sky.

He dragged deeply on his cigarette. "This used to be one of my favorite spots to camp out. Nothing better than waking up under a clear, blue sky in the pink flush of dawn with the smell of frying bacon and cornbread filling the air."

Bree came and sat beside him. "Who was cooking the bacon?"

Will took another deep drag. "This is one of

Grady's favorite spots, too. We camped up here together sometimes."

"Not anymore?"

Will stomped out the butt on the ground and flicked it. "Not anymore."

"Why not?"

"You startin' on me again, ma'am?"

"Didn't notice I'd stopped."

Will frowned. "Grady's a stubborn old codger. Never knew a man to get me so riled." He sighed. "Oh, well, he's set in his ways. Can't say I don't understand that. Pretty much set in my ways myself."

Bree studied Will thoughtfully for a few moments. "Who taught you how to handle a gun? Was it Grady?" Her gaze was shrewd.

Will leaned back fully on the ground. His cowboy hat fell down over his eyes and shaded his sun-creased features. Cushioning his hands behind his neck, he stared pensively up at the sky through the lofty branches of the aspens. "I worked on a ranch in Montana for a couple years when I was in my teens. Grady worked there, too. Evenings, he used to put on a little show for the hands—for his own amusement, really. I thought I was a hotshot at target shooting myself in those days, a real cocky kid. But Grady was something else. I near drove him crazy until he agreed to teach me some of what he knew. He was real leery at first, but I wore him down. Turned out to be a good teacher—a lot more patient than I imagined he'd be."

Will paused. "He taught me a lot." His jaw tightened imperceptibly. He rubbed at it absently. "Yeah," he repeated, a faint edge to his voice, "Grady taught me a lot, all right."

Bree looked down at him. "About target shooting—or about life in general?"

Will tipped his hat up an inch and squinted in her direction. "He taught me what being a cowboy is all about. Grady is the last of the old breed."

"No," Bree said thoughtfully, "I think you are the last of the old breed." She tilted her head, smiling. "Even if you were a vacuum cleaner salesman once upon a time."

"A what?" His face broke into a broad grin.

Bree arched a brow. "Well, that's one theory, anyway." She poked him in the chest. "And since you're bound and determined to keep your past a deep, dark secret, I suppose that theory's as good as any."

Will laughed, pulling her to him. "I suppose it is."

Bree frowned, but she allowed Will to draw her into his arms. "You're impossible."

His laughter faded, and he pressed his lips to her sweetly scented hair. "I never pretended to be otherwise."

Bree snuggled into him, relishing the mingled scents of tobacco and musk, the feel of his strong arms around her, and his warm breath against her hair. They were silent for a long while as they watched the sun rise in the calico-blue sky.

"I'd like to camp out here with you sometime," Bree said, stretching out on the grassy knoll with her eyes closed. "I'd love to wake up under the big open sky to the smell of sizzling bacon and cornbread."

"Whoa there, gal. You've got that all wrong. I'm the one who wakes up to the sizzling bacon."

"I never sizzled bacon outdoors."

Will grinned. "Bet you never spent a night sleeping under a night sky, either."

Bree opened her mouth to argue, then laughed. "Don't reckon I ever did."

He turned on his side; his hand reached out to stroke her cheek. "Reckon you never made love under an open sky, then." He trailed his fingers lightly across her parted lips.

Bree slowly, provocatively, shook her head. "Never did. How about tonight, cowboy?" She smiled. "I'll even try my hand at bacon tomorrow morning—if you're willing to teach me."

Will's eyes held tender passion. "There's a lot I'd like to teach you, tenderfoot." His hand moved down to her shirt; his fingers worked at the first button as his mouth lowered to capture hers.

Bree's hand moved over his, and she tugged it away. Will stopped in midkiss and lifted his head questioningly.

"Tonight, Will. I don't want to start something now and have to stop."

"No reason to stop."

"You know I've got an appointment with that advertising man, Greg Parker, today. He's flying out here to meet with me at eleven, and then he's going to

109

stay for the afternoon rehearsal. We really have to get back. I'm going to pick him up in Green River. I told you all about it last night."

His humorless smile did little to soften Will's features. "Last night my mind was on other things," he said. "Didn't pay attention to all that talk about New York City advertising men coming out here with their fancy ideas."

Bree grinned. "You obviously paid enough attention, Mr. Sheridan, to know he was coming out here from New York City."

Will's expression remained sullen. "Nothing wrong with the advertising the way it is now. Van Lothridge over in Green River does a damned good job."

"Sure," Bree countered, "for the local hick towns you've been playing to. But I'm working on bookings in Cheyenne, Salt Lake City, and Butte. I close those deals, and we're going to need advertising with eye-catching polish. Parker is going to help me develop an image, something that people will be able to immediately identify with the show. Don't you see, darling? Once we make a splash this way, we can begin to build on our reputation. Folks will hustle from every corner of the country to book the show. Hell, why stop here? I bet they'd go crazy for a Wild West show all over Europe. And in Japan. My God, Japan could be a gold mine." She looked expectantly at Will. "Come on, darling. Wouldn't it be grand to travel the globe together, see it all from the top of the world?" She laughed dryly. "Wouldn't it be exquisite justice?"

Will made no response. He was spreading some tobacco from his pouch onto a square of paper and rolling it with single-handed ease. He struck a wooden match on the heel of his boot and lit up, took a deep drag, and exhaled slowly.

Bree touched her hand lightly to his shoulder. "There's a lot I would love to show you, cowboy. It could be so wonderful."

Will's continued silence unnerved her. She had to keep up the one-sided conversation until she got a response from him. "The show is so good, Will! People everywhere deserve to see it. And they're going to love it—not to mention pay a good price for the privilege. Oh, I know you don't feel making a lot of money is important. But think what you could do with some real cash in your pocket! Why, you could buy yourself the finest ranch in Wyoming. You could stock it with a herd of cattle, or breed horses, or both. Why not?"

He stood without saying a word, shrugging her hand off his shoulder. "Let's get back." His voice betrayed little emotion.

"Damn it, Will!" she snapped, grabbing at his sleeve. "Isn't it time you put that steely-faced cowboy bit to rest? If you've got something to say, then say it."

Will turned slowly. Bree saw the throbbing pulse in his throat and his darkening features. "You don't get it, do you?" he asked.

Bree leaped up; her fingers still grasped his shirt. "Get what? How can I get anything? How can I understand anything when you close yourself off? How, for heaven's sake, can you get any real satisfaction from performing in these dreary backwater towns to a handful of raggedy little kids—"

Will grabbed her up so sharply, she was literally lifted off her feet. A surge of fear raced through her. She'd never seen him look so fierce. Too stunned to protest, she could only stare wide-eyed into his cobalt-blue eyes.

"I happened to have been a raggedy little kid myself. I lived in more than half those backwater towns we bring the show to." Suddenly he released her, making no effort to keep her from stumbling to the ground. "You wanted to know about my past so bad— well, all you have to do is come along to any one of those backwater towns, see any one of those kids, gal, and you'll see my past—you'll see it all."

Before Bree could respond, Will had mounted his stallion. He didn't take off immediately. First he gave her a cold, hard-edged look. "You think I'm living some sort of fantasy. You're dead wrong, Bree. You're the one stuck in fantasy. Up to now, you've made me a big part of it: your western cowboy hero. Real romantic. Well, let me tell you something. There's nothing romantic about me or my life. I'm just a simple soul without a dime to my name, bringing just a dusting of pleasure to folks who deserve plenty more. I don't suppose you could ever understand that. You, with your fancy ideas, your fancy clothes, your fancy education and high-class breeding, you want to take the show to New York to show all your well-heeled friends what a

112

big success you can be. You want to parade us around like a bunch of puppets. Well, lady, I don't let any man or any woman pull my strings. The only reason I even sold the ownership to your husband was that I was in need of hard cash at the time and I knew damned well your husband didn't care about any involvement in the operation. But I'll tell you something. If I'd had the slightest idea you were gonna show up and try to tie a noose around my neck—"

Bree got to her feet and grabbed hold of a piece of Will's horse's reins.

"Right this minute, Will Sheridan, I'd give my right arm for a noose. You deserve to be strung up for talking to me this way. I don't know why the hell you're so all-fired angry. And I resent your accusing me of not being able to understand poverty!" she shouted at him. "I certainly can understand you wanting to give disadvantaged children a chance—"

He leaned down low in the saddle; a sneering expression cut across his face. "Disadvantaged children," he said in a low hiss. "Where'd you pick up that phrase? In one of your fancy college textbooks? You probably think *disadvantaged* means not getting ice cream for dessert every night. Well, I'll tell you what it means to those kids who sit in those bleachers watching my show. It means not being sure on any particular night if there's going to be any supper on the table. Or even a table at all. Half of them have been evicted from more places than they can count.

They're not disadvantaged," he snarled, "they're *poor,* lady. Dirt-poor."

He wrenched the reins from her hands; the force of the pull set her off balance so that she stumbled to the ground. "I should have been smarter than to think a high-strung gelding could mix with an old work-horse." With those words, he pressed his heels into his horse's flanks and rode off at a breakneck speed. Bree's hands sprang to her face as a cloud of pebbles and dust struck her.

She sat stunned by the turn of events. Minutes before, she had been in Will's arms, talking about making love under the open skies, and then he was giving her a lecture about poverty.

Tears of anger and hurt stung her eyes. She stood up and dusted herself off. She didn't need any lectures. She resented Will's accusations. How dared he think she didn't understand what it was all about. Her own family wasn't exactly rolling in dough.

She swiped at the tears streaming down her cheeks. Okay, so maybe she'd never known abject poverty. Maybe she had grown up with a fair number of advantages. Was she supposed to feel guilty for having gone to a top eastern college? And for having spent most of the last three years in the lap of luxury? "Anyway, where did it all get me?" she muttered to herself. Right now, she and Will Sheridan were in the same boat. And the fact was, she enjoyed sharing that boat with him. She more than enjoyed it. He had to realize that she was in love with him. Couldn't he see how happy she had been these last three weeks?

"I've never *been* this happy, you—you jerk!" she shouted through her sobs into the silent morning.

The crunch of footsteps behind her made her twirl around, and the thought that Will was returning lightened her tearstained face.

Only it wasn't Will.

CHAPTER SEVEN

"Hate to see what happens to you, ma'am, when you're miserable, if this is how you are when you're happy."

Bree did her best to sniff back her tears as she stared bleakly at Grady.

"I am miserable," she said with a wan smile.

Grady nodded slowly.

"You know Will best, Grady. Has he always been so —so self-righteous, so—pigheaded, so damned sure he knows all the answers?"

A gentle smile crossed the old man's lips as once again he slowly nodded his head.

"Have you been here very long?" Bree asked awkwardly.

Grady grinned. "Been here all night."

Bree's cheeks reddened as she realized that, if it hadn't been for her appointment with that advertising executive today, she and Will might have spent the morning up here making love under the open sky under the watchful eye of Grady. "You might have made yourself known," she said sharply.

"Reckon I just did."

Bree's frustrated grimace was followed by a weary sigh.

Grady smiled gently. "I was only within hearin' range."

Bree looked down to her shirt; her flush deepened as she spotted the undone top button. She quickly refastened it, then closed her eyes; her thick lashes fanned her rosy-hued cheeks. "I suppose there isn't a soul on this ranch who doesn't know that Will and I have gotten close." Her cheeks were positively burning now.

Grady tipped his hat and looked off toward the mountains as Bree fidgeted with her hair. "Reckon not." He turned to her and gave her a sly smile.

"I suppose this kind of thing happens all the time. Annie says gals are always losing their hearts to Will." She could feel tears starting again and bit down hard on her lower lip.

Grady untied his brightly colored red and blue bandanna from around his neck and handed it to her. She gave him a grateful nod and wiped her eyes.

"Blow," he ordered.

She did as he said, then tucked the bandanna into her pocket. "Thanks."

Grady set himself down on the grassy knoll. "Mighty pretty spot. I always did favor the hills around these parts. Came into this world not far from here. I remember, when I was just a little tike, climbing up hills like this just to watch the covered wagons crossing those trails down there. There was such an air of excitement. Never felt nothin' else like it. All those people giving up their worldly comforts, coming out here to search for their dreams. There were plenty who called this the promised land. It was the promised land, the way I saw it. For me, it still is. Of course, things have changed a mite. But out here you can still hold on to the old ways. You can still be your own man. And that's a mighty good feeling."

Bree sat down next to Grady. "And that's the bottom line, is it? Being your own man?"

"Reckon so."

"It's something you and Will have in common. It's certainly the bottom line for him. He's going to be his own man if it means destroying everything else he has. It's a nice adage and all, Grady, but it isn't exactly realistic or practical." She hesitated. "There is such a thing as compromise, working together, bending a little."

Grady smiled at Bree as if she were a child. "Will's never been one to compromise, ma'am. He's just about the most stubborn, high-tempered cowboy I ever ran across. Next to me, that is. We're probably two of the most ornery cowboys around these parts."

"Will says you taught him what being a cowboy was all about. What did he mean?"

Grady gave her a sly look. "Will said that, did he?"

Bree arched a brow. "You know very well he did. You already admitted hearing our conversation."

Grady merely smiled. Then without answering

Bree, he took to staring off into the valley below. He was silent for a time. And then he began speaking again. "I like to come up here and think about the old days." His gaze narrowed. "Over them hills yonder used to be a little white schoolhouse." He chuckled. "Not likely to forget that place. Not with all the whuppings I suffered there. Teachers always at me for daydreaming, staring off out the window. Why, you could see cowpunchers herding cattle not fifty yards from the school. That was where I was aching to be, but my mom, she wanted me to stay in school. To make her happy, I agreed to stick it out till my twelfth birthday, but there was no holding me down till then. I didn't mean to break my word. Thing was, I had no patience with schooling. No patience with all them whuppings, either.

"Truth is, all I wanted to do was ride and drive cattle across this land. So I up and quit schoolin' when I was ten. I couldn't stay cooped up another minute. Got me a job right off. In those days, kids out here could do that. Even now, plenty youngsters quit school as soon as they turn sixteen and head out to work on one of the big ranches. The life hasn't changed all that much. I worked plenty of ranches in my day. Restless cowpuncher, I was."

He stuck a wad of chewing tobacco into his mouth, chewed silently for a while, and then heaved a deep sigh. "Real restless, I was. Always got bored staying in one spot too long. I wanted to see the country. Pretty much covered it, from Montana clear down to Mexico. In those days you could pick up your saddle, set it down on a new fence, and start working for the next outfit. I put in long, hard days. All us hands did. Everything from cow work to mending fences. Nights we'd go down to the dance halls. Some of the men hankered for a good game of cards, others for the booze. Me, I didn't gamble or drink, but I did enjoy seeing them dancin' girls. They were somethin', all right. Pretty as pictures."

Bree smiled. "I bet you were a real ladies' man in those days, Grady. Bet you stole many a dance-hall gal's heart."

"Reckon I stole a few." He laughed dryly. "Reckon more than a few stole mine." He wiped his hand across his face. "I never stayed around long enough to let the pain fester, though."

"You never married?" Bree asked.

Grady shook his head. "Came close once, but I never was exactly the marrying type. Yeah, I was restless. Been restless most of my life. Reckon it's time to think of settlin' down."

Bree stared at the old man thoughtfully. "What is it with you and Will, Grady?"

"Reckon me and Will are a lot alike. Most fellahs today think they're cowboys if they pop a big hat on their heads, grab a rope, and booze it up partying Saturday nights. Will knows what it's really like. He's worked ranches since he was knee-high to a grasshopper. That boy could ride a horse before he could walk, seems to me. And back when he was working with me

120

on the Double-O Ranch, he was a mighty impressive cowpuncher. The life was in his blood, same as me." He chuckled softly. "He's always been a heck of a show-off, too. Reckon we got that in common same as the rest."

"Will says you taught him how to shoot."

"He wanted to be Buffalo Bill, all right. Damn near as good now, I reckon. Got it into his head to do up a Wild West show while we were together at the Double-O. Wanted me to go partners with him." Grady rubbed his jaw. "I told him he was plumb loco to think I'd give up cowpunching to become a showman. Those knife-throwing stunts were just somethin' I'd done for fun pretty near all my life. Didn't see it as no profession. Tell you the truth, I didn't think Will was really gonna do it. Figured it was a boy's dream. But it stayed with him. He worked for plenty of ranches for many a year, saved every cent he could, and then up and did it."

"Annie says you joined the troupe five years ago. What made you change your mind?" Bree asked.

Grady stared at Bree for a long while without saying a word. Then he stood up. His eyes were cast off into the distance again. "Reckon he needed me," he said in a low voice. "And I reckon I owed him."

Bree's brow creased. "Why, Grady? Why'd you owe him?"

The old man turned and gave her such a thorough inspection, Bree was taken aback. Not that there was anything the least insolent or seductive about it; it was more as if he were looking straight through to her very soul.

"Don't be fooled, gal, thinking Will's nothing more than a fun-loving cowboy. He's not playacting. Not about who he is. Not about how he feels toward you. You take that serious, gal. You hear me? 'Cause I don't want to see that boy hurt no more."

Bree stared at Grady, taken aback by what he had said. Then she ran her tongue over her dry lips. "I love him, Grady."

He kept his steady gaze on her. "I love him, too." He removed his hat, wiped his forearm across his brow, and then shoved it back on. He started to head off toward a grove of aspen, but Bree caught up with him. "You didn't say why you owe him, Grady. I want to know. I think I need to know."

Grady's mouth quirked in a dry line. "He's my boy."

That statement made, it lay there like a bomb. For the first time in her life, Bree was speechless. By the time she was able to gather her wits about her, a hundred questions had popped into her mind, but Grady had disappeared into the hills.

As eager as Bree was to get more details from Grady about that bombshell, there was no time. She was already late to pick up Greg Parker in Green River, and she didn't want to greet him in a pair of worn-out jeans and a cowboy shirt. She was determined to impress Parker as the owner of one of the most promising show-business properties around. She wanted the advertising executive to smell success. As soon as she got back to her room, she changed quickly into a soft rose-colored linen dress and a pair of matching pumps. She did her best to tame her wild hair, drawing it back with an ornamental clasp at the nape of her neck. A little eye shadow, blush, and some lipstick, and she looked almost like her old self again.

She gave a quick inspection in the mirror and grimaced at her hair. "Oh, for just one visit to Henri's salon!"

Joey Ross was rehearsing alone down in the barn. When he spotted Bree, he let out a long wolf whistle.

"You look terrific!"

Bree grinned. "You sound surprised."

Joey flushed. "Hey, no. I mean, you always look great, but I never saw you all dressed up fancy before."

Bree could have reminded him of that first afternoon when she'd arrived at the ranch in her even fancier Anne Klein suit, but she reminded herself of the condition she had been in, to say nothing of the outfit, when Will had gotten her there in his Jeep.

"Where are you off to?" Joey asked.

"I've got to pick up a friend in Green River," Bree said, deciding this was no time to go into her plans and negotiations with Parker. "Will mentioned awhile back that I could use the Jeep if I needed to get into town for anything. I saw it out there earlier this morning."

"Still there. Key's in the ignition."

Bree smiled. "Well, see you later." She started across the barn, then came to a stop and glanced back over her shoulder at Joey. "Hey, I think this is going to be a great summer."

Joey laughed. "They're always great."

Bree nodded, and her smile gave way to a vague uneasiness. Will was right. It seemed everyone in the company was perfectly happy with the way things were. Well, she decided with a firm set to her lovely jaw, they'll be even happier when they're all big stars in a smash hit production.

By the time Bree arrived at the small airport outside Green River, Greg Parker had been waiting nearly a half hour. He didn't look happy about it, but as Bree hurried over, his eyes fell on her and his frown faded instantly. Bree recognized the look on the advertising executive's face. He'd quickly decided she was worth waiting for.

It was the superficial approval that so many of the men she knew in New York were adept at extending, but right now that smile buoyed her spirits and her optimism. She took a deep breath of anticipation, introduced herself, and offered her hand.

Greg Parker had a firm grip and a deep baritone voice. He was an old beau of Bree's friend Grace. Fortunately for Bree, Grace and Greg had remained on good terms after their affair had run its course. Greg had consented to fly out here to see the show in rehearsal and meet with Bree thanks to Grace's persuasive skills.

Bree was nervous that Grace might have given Parker the impression that she had a lot more money to spend on advertising and public relations than she did. She was going to have to convince Parker that although they would have to start small, his agency stood to make a real killing once their reputation started to spread and bigger deals were cut.

"How about some lunch in town?" Bree suggested after the introductions. "It would be quieter in a restaurant than back at the ranch. Rehearsal starts at four, but there's always a lot of commotion while they set up."

Greg Parker was a tall, well-dressed man in his mid-thirties with shrewd brown eyes, immaculately styled sandy blond hair, an attractive smile, and a distinctly cosmopolitan manner. He looked about as in place in the Green River scene as a cowpuncher leading his herd down Fifth Avenue would.

Holden House was the best restaurant Green River had to offer. It was also the most expensive, which also meant it tended to be a lot less crowded than Deke's Diner and the Triple E Bar and Grill. The waitress found Bree and Greg a pleasant private table by the window.

After the waitress took their drink order—a Manhattan for Greg and a beer on tap for Bree, for which she'd acquired a taste since she'd gone "western"—Greg leaned back in his chair, his arms crossed, and surveyed Bree with a measuring gaze.

Bree smiled. "Let me guess what's on your mind.

You're wondering"—she leaned slightly forward—"what a nice girl like me is doing in a place like this."

Greg laughed. "You're not only beautiful but a mind reader as well."

"When you see the show, you'll have the answer to your question, Mr. Parker."

"Call me Greg."

"As long as you promise not to call me ma'am."

"Huh?"

Bree giggled. "Sorry. Private joke."

The drinks came. Greg took one sip of his Manhattan, grimaced, and then glanced over at Bree. "Now I see why you ordered a beer."

"You learn fast out here."

He moved his drink aside. "So tell me about yourself, Bree."

"Don't you mean tell you about the Sheridan Wild West Show?"

"In time. First I want to know about the lady who runs the show. Grace says you're something else."

Bree's aquamarine eyes sparkled. "I bet she did."

"Really. She's a fan of yours. Says you have a lot of guts." His attractive smile was full of admiration and approval.

"And only a little cash."

The warmth faded from Greg's smile.

Bree took a deep breath and gazed at him frankly. "Look, Greg, I think I'd better lay all my cards on the table. I know your firm handles some of the biggest accounts going. The Sheridan Wild West Show

126

wouldn't rate more than peanuts against any one of them at the moment." She put a lot of emphasis on the last phrase. "With the right approach and plenty of hard work, I guarantee we can make it to the top. Western is in, Greg. All over the country. Clothing, furniture—even Hollywood is back into horse operas. The time is ripe, and I've got a property that can really offer something. This troupe is for real. I mean, true home-on-the-range types, with talent pouring out of their ears. And the star of the show—" Bree's voice caught. She took a sip of beer, realized that her hand was trembling, and set the mug down on the table. "He's terrific."

"Oh?" Greg's voice held a questioning note.

Bree felt her cheeks warm. "I mean, he's got star written all over him."

"He's that good, huh?" His skepticism had not been assuaged.

Bree was saved from further discomfort by the arrival of the waitress. "Shall we order?"

Greg didn't look as if he were excited by the prospect, but he smiled politely. "Why don't you order for both of us? Whatever your favorite is . . ." He let the sentence hang.

"I haven't eaten here before, to tell you the truth." Bree looked up at the waitress. "What do you recommend?"

"Never go wrong with the ribs."

Bree smiled. "Sounds good to me." She glanced over at Greg, who nodded his agreement.

When the waitress left, Greg returned to the subject of Will Sheridan.

"So what's this guy like?"

It was hard to deal with the tumultuous emotions she was feeling about Will, much less talk about him to a total stranger, even though she knew that selling Parker on Will was vital. Will was the heart and soul of the show. "I thought you wanted to know about me," Bree said, mustering a coquettish tone.

Greg laughed good-naturedly. "Very slick maneuver. Hey, I think we could use you in the firm."

"The point is, Greg, I could use you—badly. We need to launch an advertising campaign that will make people sit up and notice. And if we're going to hit the market I'm aiming for, that campaign has got to be as slick as they come. And you're the man to do it. I've seen your work. The campaigns you ran for the Manhattan Mime Troupe and the Red Apple Circus were as good as they come."

Greg was pleased by the compliment but wary nonetheless. "Those shows had already established a pretty good following by the time I stepped in." He hesitated. "And to put it bluntly, Bree, they had a fair-size budget for advertising."

Bree dazzled him with a Miss America smile. "What I'm offering you that those other shows didn't is a real challenge, Greg."

Greg grinned. "The question is, Bree, am I game for taking on a real challenge?"

There was no avoiding the implication in Greg's seductive tone. It severely dampened Bree's beauty-contest-winning smile.

Spotting Will Sheridan standing ten yards away from the window where she and Greg were having their cozy tête-à-tête further doused it. More accurately, the harsh, set features of his face and the narrowing of his blue eyes as they met hers through the glass picture window doused it.

"Speak of the devil," Bree mumbled.

Greg followed Bree's gaze. He let out a low whistle. "Let me guess: the cowboy with star quality."

Bree's gaze had not broken with Will's. She nodded imperceptibly.

"Oh, God," Bree muttered under her breath when she saw Will head toward the restaurant. How to destroy all hope of getting Greg to take the account in one easy step. The last thing she wanted was for the two men to meet before Greg got to see how great the show was. She had hoped that the advertising executive would become so excited by the performance that he'd be amenable to coping with a recalcitrant star. On top of everything else, Will was now very likely still fuming over the spat they'd had this morning. Bree herself had almost forgotten how angry she was at Will; learning that he was Grady's son had stunned the fury right out of her.

As Will entered the dining room, Bree experienced that familiar sharp surge of desire that she felt whenever she as much as looked at him. But as he neared the table, his frosty blue eyes tempered her heat.

"Will, I'd like you to meet Greg Parker. Greg, this is Will Sheridan." She could hear archness in her voice and knew that Will would stamp phoniness right across it, but she was too nervous to soften the tone.

Will pulled a chair up to the table without an invitation. Bree expected Greg to look disappointed, but she was astounded to find him beaming from ear to ear. She gave him a bemused smile, but Greg was too busy sizing Will up to notice.

"You look about as authentic as they come, cowboy," Greg said, shaking Will's hand in a friendly, enthusiastic fashion. "If I take your show on, we'll definitely use you for personal appearances. Man, you'd have those teeny-boppers rushing to the ticket booths in droves." He glanced over at Bree, whose honey-hued complexion had turned almost white. If only she'd warned Greg about Will! She clenched her teeth together and waited for Will to explode.

But she should have known by now that Will Sheridan never did what she expected him to. Instead of having an apoplectic fit, Will gave Parker a wry smile, then gazed insolently at Bree. "Maybe we ought to deck Bree out, too. We could make personal appearances together." Will leaned toward Bree. Only she could see the cruel twist of his lips. "I could have her stick a cigarette between her lips, and then I'd blindfold myself and shoot it out of her mouth. That ought to drive the teeny-boppers wild."

"As long as you don't miss the target," Greg said, oblivious to the underlying tension.

Will was still staring at Bree with cobalt-blue eyes. "I only miss when I mean to."

Greg finally caught the icy drift. "If I've stepped into the middle of something here—"

Before he could finish his sentence, the waitress deposited two plates of steaming-hot ribs onto the table and a mug of beer for Will.

"Thanks, sugar," Will drawled. "Some gals know what a man wants without him having to say a word."

The waitress, a pretty young brunette, beamed. "You looked like you needed to wet your whistle when you walked in, Will."

As she started off, Will called out to her. "I left a ticket to the show for you up at the desk. We open in Green River in two weeks."

The waitress waved a thanks, and Bree leaned forward. "We do? I didn't see Green River in the schedule."

"That's because the schedule only lists paying spots. We always throw in a free show in town to start off the season."

Bree's eyes narrowed. "We do?"

Greg fidgeted with his tie. "Not a smart business move."

Will's features darkened to a frown. "I don't reckon it's a business move at all, smart or otherwise. We always open in Green River, and the proceeds always go to charity. That's the way it is."

Bree compressed her lips. It was hard to keep her mouth shut, but she knew this was no time for a spar-

131

ring match with a master. She parted her lips only to take a bite of the ribs. As she started chewing, her mouth felt as if it had been attacked by fire. She gasped, then broke into a coughing fit.

Will grinned, lifted her beer, and put it to her lips. "Here, ma'am. To put out the blaze."

Bree shoved his hand away, which sent the mug flying.

"Now look . . . what . . . you . . . did!" she sputtered in between coughs.

Greg seemed at a complete loss. He looked as if he would rather be anywhere else on earth at the moment.

Then Will rose from his seat and unceremoniously pulled Bree out of hers, grasped her wrists, and lifted her arms high above her head. As angry as she was at this manhandling, the maneuver did get her coughing under control.

"There, that's better," Will drawled. He set her back down into her seat with the same rough manner he'd used to get her out of it.

Bree was seething, but when she saw the painful discomfort in Greg's face, her rage mixed with anguish as she imagined all her hopes and dreams going down the drain.

Only Will seemed perfectly at ease. "Well, I'll leave you two to dig into those ribs and get on with your business meetin'. I've got to get our flyers printed up across the street at Van's shop for the Green River performance."

As Will stood up, he glided his beer mug over to Greg, then glanced down at the advertising executive's as-yet-untouched plate of ribs. With a broad smile on his face, he said, "Here, have this on me. You're gonna need it." He ran his deep blue eyes over Bree. "Believe me."

Bree watched in silent fury as Will swaggered out. Then she looked over at Greg with an apologetic smile on her face.

"I'm sorry," she said softly. "I guess I should have warned you that Will Sheridan isn't an easy man to deal with."

A slow smile curved Greg Parker's lips. "That's got to be the biggest understatement I've heard all year." He shoved aside his plate of ribs. "But I'll tell you something, Bree. You were right. The guy's definitely got charisma with a capital C. Dress him up Presley style, arrange some personal appearances, get him an aftershave lotion or a deodorant commercial to do—hell, splash his photo all over the media to plug the Wild West show—" He came to a sudden breathless halt. "He really is good, isn't he?"

Bree laughed. "He's the last of a breed, Parker. And one of the best, believe me."

CHAPTER EIGHT

When Bree showed up with Greg for the rehearsal, the barn was empty except for Joey Ross. It was almost four. Ever since her arrival in Green River, the troupe had started rehearsals like clockwork at four o'clock sharp. Bree looked around. The stage set hadn't even been pulled out yet. She glanced at Greg. He looked baffled and more than a little irritated.

"What's going on?" he asked sharply, brushing a stray piece of hay from his jacket sleeve.

Bree wanted an answer to that question herself. She had a suspicion that Will had called off today's rehearsal out of spite. He must have figured that if Greg Parker didn't get to see the show, he wasn't likely to work out a deal with Bree.

"I don't understand it," she lied. "Must be a problem with one of the horses or something. I'm sure it'll be all right. I'll check."

She crossed the wide barn to where Joey Ross was sitting on a bale of hay looking like a cowboy who'd just had his favorite horse sent off to the glue factory.

134

Only it wasn't a missing horse that was troubling him.

"What's wrong?" Bree asked him anxiously. "Where is everybody? Why aren't you all getting ready for the rehearsal?"

Joey tipped his Stetson way back on his head. "No rehearsal," he muttered glumly. "Maggie cleared out."

"Cleared out? But why?"

"Don't ask me." He shrugged. "I swear I'll never understand women. Maggie McPhee most of all."

Bree glanced over across the barn to Greg. He had begun pacing—definitely not a good sign.

She turned her attention back to Joey. "Well, where did she go?"

"Beats me."

Bree felt her anger rising. "How could she just up and abandon the show? Doesn't she realize how much we all depend on each other?"

"Maggie doesn't seem to realize much of anything," he muttered, his jaw twitching.

Bree crossed her arms in front of her. "Well, she must have had a reason. Exactly what happened?"

Joey frowned. "You're asking the wrong cowboy."

Bree felt her whole body stiffen. "And who should I ask?"

Joey pulled his hat back down over his eyes and leaned back against the barn wall. "Ask Will."

As if she hadn't already figured that out for herself. Her eyes narrowed. She'd known as soon as she walked into the empty barn that Will Sheridan was behind the problem.

Bree's blue-green eyes looked like ice. She shook an irate finger at Joey. "You can bet I'll ask him!" she said emphatically, then tried to calm her rage before she got to Greg. It didn't help matters when Joey called out, "You can ask him, but I doubt you'll get an answer. When I tried, it was like talking to a stone wall."

Warily, Greg eyed Bree. "Well, what's happening? Is there going to be a rehearsal or not?"

She squeezed Greg's arm. "Wait here. You're going to see a rehearsal today, with or without Maggie McPhee."

Greg caught her sleeve as she turned to leave. "Who's Maggie McPhee?"

Bree shrugged, giving Greg a smile that she hoped would inspire confidence. "It's not important. Just give me a few minutes. This won't take long to straighten out."

"Listen, Bree," Greg said, "I've got to catch the seven o'clock plane out of Green River this evening. It's the only one that'll link up with my nine o'clock flight out of Casper. I've got to be back in New York for an important morning meeting. I just can't—"

Bree cut him off. "You'll make your plane, Greg, I promise. And you're going to see the best damned rehearsal the Sheridan Wild West Show has ever put on. Just sit tight." She glanced back at Joey on her way out of the barn. "Hey, cowboy. Pull up another bale of hay for the tenderfoot."

Hurrying down the path to the ranch, Bree ran into Annie.

"Did Maggie show up?" Bree asked hopefully.

"Nope." Annie looked less morose than Joey but no less resigned. "I have a feeling she'll turn up again one of these days after she cools down a bit."

"Annie, what happened?"

Annie's eyes narrowed. "That's just what I went to find out. Will gave me one of his lazy smiles and shrugged. I swear, that man can be more obstinate than a mule."

"Tell me about it," Bree muttered.

Annie gave her a shrewd look. "Maybe you can tell me what went wrong. This morning I saw you and Will head off on your horses looking like a couple of lovesick cows, and then Will came flying back down here a couple hours later looking like a mean-minded bull breathing hellfire. I've seen Will hot-tempered before, but this time he was positively burning." Annie shook her head. "Most of us know better than to deal with Will when he gets in one of those states. But Maggie—well, I guess Maggie saw it as an opportunity to step right in and try to soothe his hurt. But that would be like pouring salt on his wounds. That gal has no sense when it comes to Will. Not that Maggie ever has any sense when it comes to men. She can't even see that poor Joey's aching for some of her soothing."

"Where's Will? Is he back at the ranch?"

Annie chuckled. "That man is a devil. He's there, all right, sitting in front of the fire, looking as pleased with himself as could be. When I asked him what we're gonna do about Maggie, he told me not to worry about it, saying what I already know, that Maggie'll turn up soon enough. Or else he'll find someone to take her place before we open Green River." Annie made a *tsk* sound, clicking her tongue against the roof of her mouth. "Just like he keeps telling me he'll find someone to take my place so I can stop being Grady's dartboard. But he doesn't even try anymore, 'cause Grady only scares off whoever he finds."

"Well, if he doesn't find someone to take Maggie's place, I will." Then, realizing the unlikeliness of that prospect, she added, "Or we'll manage without her." She grasped Annie's arm. "Right now, gather everyone up and tell them that I want to have a dress rehearsal down at the barn in fifteen minutes sharp." Bree bit down on her lip. "Oh, God, I hope Grady hasn't wandered off, too."

"No, Grady's still around. But—"

"No buts," Bree said firmly.

"Well, I'll tell the others. But you're gonna have a time convincing Will there's gonna be a rehearsal. I sure as heck wouldn't want to order Will Sheridan around in the mood he's in today. One minute he's smilin', the next he's hissin' like a rattler. Can't tell what's gonna follow."

Bree drew her shoulders back and gave her head a

regal shake. "I'd be only too happy to deal with Mr. Will Sheridan and his multifaceted moods."

"My, oh, my." Annie chuckled. "Something tells me sparks are gonna be flying out of that ranch like firecrackers on the Fourth of July."

Bree's eyes flickered with a determined glint as she left Annie laughing and headed for the ranch.

When she got there, she was so caught up in what she was going to tell Will that she forgot about the loose board on the porch steps. Her heel caught, and she went flying forward with a shriek; her hands shot out to break her fall.

Sprawled out on the porch, cursing under her breath, she was examining her bruised hands and the jagged rip along the seam of her dress when Will ambled up and looked down at her.

"Been expecting you," he said nonchalantly.

Bree glared up at him.

"Need a hand?"

"Not one of yours," she snapped, and struggled to rise, only to discover that the heel of her pump was jammed solid under the splintered board.

Will, seeing the problem, made a move to help her.

Bree's hand shot up, stopping him. "I told you, I don't need your brand of help, Mr. Sheridan."

"Suit yourself . . . ma'am." He leaned casually against a newel post.

Bree gritted her teeth and extricated her foot from her shoe. Then she got into a sitting position and leaned forward to try to pry the shoe loose. Just when she got a good grip on it, a splinter of wood jabbed her palm. She let out a scream and let go of the shoe.

Will bent over her as she tried to remove the splinter. Without asking, he grabbed her hand.

"Gonna need a tweezers. Got one inside," he said, examining the damage. "Pretty scraped up, too. We'll have to clean you up."

Through teeth clenched half in rage and half to keep from crying in pain, she said, "I'll clean myself up, thank you."

But Will's grip on her wrist was as strong as a handcuff. He had her up on her feet before she could protest.

She took a limping step, then remembered that she was minus one pump.

"My shoe."

Will grinned. "You can get it later."

Bree's jaw twitched in anger, but she limped defiantly into the house. Will slammed the door behind them and then released her.

"There should be a tweezers around here somewhere." He walked over to the kitchen and rummaged through the drawers.

Bree stood in the center of the room trying not to wince in pain.

"Found one," he said, holding up the tweezers victoriously.

"I can do it myself," Bree said as he came toward her.

Will paid no attention and grabbed her hand. Bree

didn't protest. She wasn't much good at operations, even minor ones.

As Will gently probed the tender area, Bree looked at him in profile. "What did you say to Maggie that made her take off?" Her tone was sharp, but as she stood breathing in Will's musky scent, she was agonizingly aware of his strong masculine presence that, no matter what her mood, had a dizzying effect on her.

Will gave her a quick glance and smiled rakishly. "Nothin' much."

Bree let out a cry as he extracted the splinter.

"Did I hurt you?" He was still holding her hand, but the grip was no longer viselike. He brought her palm to his lips and kissed the wound tenderly.

Bree swallowed. "My mother used to do that when I was small." Only she had never felt this way when her mother kissed her.

Will led her across the room to the kitchen sink, turned on the taps, and brought her hands under the spray. As she washed gingerly, he opened a tube of first-aid cream. After she dried her hands, she offered her wounded palm to him without argument and let him gently apply the cream and a bandage.

He didn't release her hand.

Bree's eyes met his. "You must have said something to Maggie to make her take off." Her voice was quivery.

A crooked smile curved his lips, and he gave a careless shrug. "Sometimes it's what a man doesn't say that makes a woman see red." His voice was seductively low.

"And what didn't you say?" Bree's voice was now husky as well as quivery.

Will gave her a lingering look; then with a slow, deliberate move he let his fingers slide up her arm. He released his hold, but his blue eyes still held her captive, mesmerizing her. "How'd that eastern dude like his ribs?"

Bree's eyes narrowed. "He wasn't fool enough to try them. Which brings us to the subject at hand, Mr. Sheridan," she said, stepping back and nearly stumbling because she'd forgotten she was still minus one shoe.

Will's hand darted out and steadied her. His other hand came up and smoothed her cinnamon hair, which fell in wild waves in every direction because her barrette had come off when she fell on the steps.

"You stormed off the hill this morning fit to be tied." Bree's hand moved unconsciously to her chest to steady the erratic beating of her racing heart.

"We do set each other off, don't we?" His fingers moved down over her cheekbone to the corner of her mouth, where they lingered. "You make life difficult for me, ma'am."

"You weren't pleasant back at the restaurant with Mr. Parker."

Will's blue eyes twinkled. "Reckon I wasn't."

"Well, although Mr. Parker didn't think much of

142

the cuisine of Green River or your manners, he thought you were simply fabulous otherwise."

Will grinned. "One of those, is he? Thought he looked a little swishy."

Bree's jaw tightened; her anger gave her the strength to break free of Will's hypnotic hold over her. "He is not one of 'those.' Anything but. He happened to think I was pretty fabulous, too. And he does not look 'swishy.' He is a perfectly acceptable-looking man!" Bree said hotly.

"Acceptable, huh?" Will's lips curled upward in a sardonic smile. "From what I could see, you were finding Mr. Parker more than acceptable."

Bree took in a steadying breath. "So that's it! You were jealous."

"Of Mr. Perfectly Acceptable-Looking Parker? Not on your life, ma'am."

"Will, this is ridiculous and unfair. Greg Parker took time out from a busy schedule to fly out here and see a rehearsal. I insist that he see it, with or without Maggie McPhee."

Will gave a careless shrug. "Can't imagine how. Maggie's a key player in our final number. Without her the act will fall flat."

"Let Annie take her place."

Will chuckled. "Annie? Bree honey, think for a minute. Have you ever seen Annie Taggart on a horse since you've been here?" Before Bree could answer, Will went on. "You haven't. And the reason is, Annie has had a downright aversion to horses since she was thrown by one when she was a young girl."

Bree sighed. "Great. This is really great." Tears spiked her eyes. "I know you don't give a damn about any of this." She looked up beseechingly. "But couldn't you just try for once in your life to compromise?" She sniffed. "Oh, I know the cowboy credo. You've got to be your own man. Grady gave me the whole lecture. He also told me . . ." Bree hesitated.

Will's eyes narrowed. "What did he tell you?"

Bree's expression turned tender. "That he's your father."

She waited for a response from Will, any response, but he didn't say a word. His enigmatic expression gave no clue to his feelings.

Bree tried to draw his eyes to hers with no luck. "I guess it really must have been . . . tough for you . . . growing up," Bree stammered nervously.

Turning to her, he met her gaze unflinchingly. Still not a word, though.

"I mean"—Bree tried to go on—"being . . ."

"Illegitimate?" A sardonic smile crossed Will's mouth. "See, ma'am, I know those big words, too. *Illegitimate, underprivileged.* Heck, honey, I reckon I could come up with a whole slew of fancy words. How about *underachiever, truant, delinquent, troublemaker.* Well, the last ain't so fancy, but what the hell. I suppose Grady told you all about my reckless youth."

Bree shook her head slowly. "No, he didn't tell me anything about your youth. He just told me that being

144

a cowboy was in your blood, same as him. He said that heading up a Wild West show was something you wanted to do ever since those days when you worked together at the ranch."

"You mean the place where I finally tracked my wayward daddy down." Will's voice held a note of wistful bitterness. Then he gave a careless shrug, as if he realized he was giving too much away. "Hell, it was a long time back. Water under the bridge, as they say. Reckon we've made our peace as best we can."

Bree smiled, but there was a deep ache for Will behind it. All the hurt, the abandonment, and the rage he must have gone through! No wonder he's so proud, so defiant, and so determined to be his own man, she thought.

"He told me one other thing," Bree said softly.

Will's expression became veiled once more. "What was that?" he asked hoarsely.

Bree clasped her trembling hands together. She looked up at him with wide, glistening eyes. "He told me he . . . loves you." Bree's voice faltered. "And I told him . . . I love you, too, Will."

She waited for a response; the ache inside her grew. Grady had all but said he believed that Will loved her. She longed for it to be true. But Will stood there silently, and Bree felt more confused and unhappy than she ever had before. Finally, unable to bear the silence another moment, she turned away. Tears rolled down her cheeks. "I'll go tell Parker . . ."

"Tell him we'll be set to go in ten minutes."

Bree swung around, her face tear-streaked. "Do you mean it, Will?" she asked breathlessly. She searched his face carefully as she pressed her hand to her chest to still her heart.

He smiled his best cowboy smile.

"Oh, Will!" She ran to him and flung her arms around him, hugged herself against him; tears still ran down her cheeks.

He had no trouble finding her lips—no trouble at all. Bree felt heat radiating from his body as he kissed her. His mouth did wonderful things to her, his teeth gently nibbled, and then his tongue danced over her lips and dipped into her mouth.

Bree arched into him, breathing in the faint aroma of tobacco and Will's own musky masculine scent. A shudder of longing ran through her as she answered his passion greedily.

They kissed until they were both breathless.

"Hey"—Will grinned—"we've got a show to put on, you and I. Reckon we'll have to save this finale for later." He gave her a playful swat on her beautifully shaped rear.

"Right," Bree murmured wistfully, "the show must go on." She glanced down at her ruined dress. "Do you think I'll have time to change?"

"Heck, honey, you *have* to change," Will drawled. "Can't very well do your part in that outfit."

Bree looked up sharply at Will. "My part?" she asked warily.

"Like I said before, Annie can't take Maggie's place. You're the only one left."

Bree backed up, still hobbling on one shoe. "Oh, no, Will. No! I couldn't."

"Sure you can. You ride like you were born in the saddle."

"Ride. Oh, I can ride, I can ride just fine. But I can't do those stunts Maggie does with Joey. You know I can't." She hobbled back a second step. "There's got to be another solution."

Will walked up to her and placed his arms lightly, caressingly, on her shoulders. "Reckon this is our chance to compromise, ma'am. Unless you want to tell your fancy eastern advertising executive that he's gonna have to come back when Maggie shows up."

Bree's eyes narrowed. "You know very well, Mr. Will Sheridan, that I'm not going to do that." She shifted her stance onto her shoed foot. Steeling herself, she said firmly, "Okay. I'll do it." Her voice wavered. "I don't know quite how I'll do it—"

Will kissed her mouth lightly. "You'll be great. Just give it your best shot."

"I'll try," Bree said weakly. Then she opened the front door and stepped out. "I just might die trying," she mumbled, hobbling onto the porch.

Will moved past her and pulled her missing shoe from between the splintered boards of the step.

"Here you go, Cinderella." He winked saucily. "Get a move on, now. Your steed awaits." He chuckled softly.

"Oh, this is giving you no end of amusement, cowboy." She jabbed his chest sharply. "You just make sure you give it your best shot out there, too."

Sticking her foot into her shoe, she strode off with a determined step.

Ten minutes later, she stood in front of her mirror scrutinizing herself in Maggie McPhee's low-cut, waist-cinching calico dress. Bree's determination had taken a sharp decline.

"I can't do this."

Annie Taggart smiled. "You look pretty as a picture."

"*Now*—now I look pretty as a picture. How am I going to look after I go hurling off one of those rooftops or get my foot caught in a stirrup while Joey's horse drags my poor tattered body along the ground? I won't be looking very pretty then, I reckon." Her mouth set in a tight line. "I swear, I think Will did this on purpose. I bet he drove Maggie off intentionally so I'd have to go out there this afternoon and make an absolute fool of myself in front of Greg Parker."

"Don't worry about a thing," Annie said, heading out the door of the bedroom.

Bree didn't even notice Annie had gone. "Make a fool of myself? How optimistic can I get? I'll be lucky if the only thing I do is make a complete fool of myself."

Her head jerked up toward the doorway as she heard a very masculine throat clearing. When she saw it was Will and that they were alone, she attempted a brave smile.

Will smiled back at her. "Everything okay? No last-minute jitters?"

"No." She knew she had responded too quickly.

"Great. We're almost ready to roll. Three minutes to curtain time."

More likely three minutes to "curtains," Bree thought morosely.

Will walked over. "You look terrific."

Bree offered a grim thanks.

"Hey, tenderfoot," he said softly, cupping her chin and tilting her head up. "You don't have to go through with this."

"Yes, I do," she said stoically, "if for no other reason, Mr. Will Sheridan, than to prove to you how important all this is to me."

Will smiled tenderly. "Reckon I already know that."

He lifted Bree to her feet. Cupping her neck, he pulled her closer and let his lips brush the corner of her mouth.

"Showtime!" Annie called up from the bottom of the stairs.

Will released Bree reluctantly.

She inhaled slowly.

"You ready?" he asked softly.

Bree compressed her lips and nodded valiantly.

"Let's go then."

"You go on ahead. I just need to check my

makeup." And, she added silently, get my knees under control so they stop knocking against each other.

"You sure?" Will gave her a close look.

"I'm sure," she said in a voice that rang with far more certainty than she was feeling.

Will crossed the room and started out the door. But he came to an abrupt halt and glanced back at Bree. "Reckon you're the most stubborn little vixen I ever did run across." He paused for a moment, inhaling roughly. "Reckon that's one of the reasons I love you." Seeing her stunned expression, Will laughed softly. "Break a leg, ma'am," he said as he continued out the door, walking with a free and easy step, full of grace and confidence.

Bree stood transfixed. Then slowly her mouth curved into a wide smile. She crossed her arms over her chest and hugged herself. "That man," she murmured. "I swear, he's impossible." She laughed. "Reckon that's one of the reasons I love him."

Her knees were no longer knocking. Bree strode out of the room, filled with optimism and joy that wouldn't have quit even if she had been about to face her "final curtain."

CHAPTER NINE

As Joey Ross dragged her around the stage set en route to their daring aerial walk along the rooftops, Bree realized that she had never before experienced real terror.

This was a first. And definitely a first she could have lived without, she thought. Gladly.

"Relax," Joey said.

Bree would have liked to tell him what she thought of his advice, but her heart was pounding so hard, she was sure it would leap right out of her chest. And her breathing was so shallow, she was afraid she was going to hyperventilate at any moment. Well, no one could say she wasn't playing the part of the terrified frontier bank teller to the hilt.

When she got to the first step leading to the roof ledge, Bree froze. "I see spots before my eyes, Joey. I'm never going to make it," she gasped in between theatrical screams that had a ring of authenticity.

"Believe me"—Joey laughed—"you'll make it fine." To Bree's ears, the sound of his laughter through the bandanna covering his mouth held a diabolical note.

"Why did I ever agree to this?" Bree moaned as Joey nudged her up the metal stairs behind the set. "I'm going to strangle Will for doing this to me—that is, if I live."

Joey squeezed her shoulder. "It's not as bad as you're imagining. Fact is, I bet you're gonna feel mighty silly in a minute."

"I'll take that bet," Bree said with a gasp as Joey's arm came around her waist and he hoisted her bandit-fashion up with him onto the roof ledge of the stage set.

Not until he set her down did Bree realize what Joey was talking about. The ledge, which from below looked to be no more than a couple of inches wide at most, was really closer to twelve inches. It was still not Bree's choice for a place to take a stroll, but she had to admit that she felt enormous relief. So much so that she almost forgot to keep up her screams.

But she also forgot, until she heard the whinnying of Joey's trusty steed a good fifteen feet below, that there were new terrors ahead.

Joey felt her body stiffen in fright. "I've done this a couple hundred times, Bree."

Bree refused to move. Below, the horse started to sound very impatient. "I don't care if you've done it a million times," Bree said, trembling. "I've never in my life leaped off a roof onto a horse. Do you hear me? Never."

"Hey, come on, Bree! You don't want to stop the show just when we're really flying, do you?"

"*Flying* is a poor word choice, Joey."

"Come on, Bree," Joey said, glancing over his shoulder. "The sheriff's gonna catch up to us in another couple of seconds."

"Okay, okay," she muttered, realizing that, terrified though she might be, pride and the fact that Greg Parker and Will were watching her forced her to take those last few steps to the end.

"Just leave it to me," Joey murmured confidently.

As if she had much choice.

He lifted her up in his arms and prepared for his leap. "Come on! Loosen up. You're stiff as a board."

"In another moment I may be stiff as a stiff," she moaned as Joey tightened his hold. She shut her eyes; terror gripped her with an even stronger hold as she and Joey literally went off the deep end.

The landing wasn't gentle, but Bree had to admit that Joey suffered a lot more of the impact than she did.

"Atta girl," Joey whispered, even though she'd done nothing more than squeeze her eyes shut, take a deep breath, and hold on to him for dear life. "Now all you have to do is sit tight. Will told me we could skip the duet stunts. I'll just do my routine."

"How big of him," Bree muttered dryly, but she had to admit that a certain headiness had come with her great sense of relief simply for having survived.

Things went swimmingly after that—until the moment before Joey had to take his fall, leaving Will to rescue her from her runaway horse.

"You're gonna have to let go of the reins, Bree, as soon as I drop," Joey told her as the pop of a blank whizzed by them, taking Joey's Stetson with it.

"You mean the reins I happen to be desperately gripping?" she moaned as they circled the arena at a brisk canter.

"Don't worry. Cobby here won't throw you." He patted the horse's flanks. "He's used to this routine."

"He may be used to it, but I'm not," Bree cried. She glanced over Joey's shoulder and saw Will, her brave cowboy, on his white charger advancing on them.

"Just lean off to your left. Make it look like you're gonna fall. It adds a lot of drama."

"I'm about to get trampled to death," she shrieked, "and the man wants drama!"

The next moment, Will shot off another blank. The sound of the pop brought new terror to her heart. This was it.

Joey gave her waist a quick, supportive squeeze, then tumbled in skillful acrobatic style to the ground.

Whether Bree would have been brave enough to let go of the reins as Joey had ordered became moot because, when Joey fell, he conveniently took the reins halfway with him, which sent Bree's lifeline flying over Cobby's head and completely out of her reach.

On cue, the horse picked up speed once Joey dropped. This was the moment when Bree was supposed to scream for help at the top of her lungs. She put her heart into it; they probably heard her in Cleveland.

The whole time she was slipping farther and farther to the left, she was thinking, What am I doing here? Why am I doing this? Why didn't I listen to Grace? But the question most prominent in her mind and the one that had the most impact was, What if Will doesn't rescue me in time?

Thank God, she thought, as Will and his trusty charger picked up speed. Never had Bree imagined that the sound of pounding hoofbeats could be so comforting.

"Just a little more of a dip!" Will called to her. He was almost at her side.

"Are you serious?" she screamed back hotly.

"A lawman's always serious." He grinned. "Trust me."

Taking a deep breath and praying it wouldn't be her last, Bree let herself slip another couple of inches to the left. She clung with one hand to the saddle. Everyone flashed by her at a dizzying speed—Greg Parker, Joey, and the rest of the troupe. Gravity drew her closer to the ground every second.

Out of the corner of her eye she saw Will extend his hand toward her. Just when she thought salvation was in sight, he intentionally pulled in his reins so that her horse moved ahead, taking her out of reach.

"Will!" she shrieked as he caught up with her again, once more reaching out for her.

He was smiling broadly. The woman had guts, he thought, even though she was scared half out of her mind. There was no denying that. Guts, beauty, and determination—a winning combination, he had to admit. No wonder he'd been unable to resist her.

Bree almost released her hold on the saddle too soon, but she was so relieved to feel Will's arm around her that she couldn't think very clearly. Will shouted at her not to let go until he had a better grip. Then came the breathless moment when Will swung her midair from her horse onto his. It was the longest moment of her life. When at last he had her safe in his arms and positioned in front of him so she sat securely sidesaddle, Bree let out a long, shaky breath.

Will squeezed her tightly, pride and satisfaction glowing on his face. "How're you doin', tenderfoot?" he asked; his large, strong fingers were spread across her ribcage.

"Never . . . again," Bree stammered. "Never—do you hear me, Will Sheridan? Never."

Will laughed as he brought his horse to a trot for the final circle around the arena. "You were terrific! Just listen to the crowd cheering you."

Only then did Bree become aware of the cheers and whistles from the troupe, who'd all gathered together to watch the finale. They were clapping wildly, and Greg Parker joined in with great enthusiasm.

Bree had been so caught up in sheer survival that she'd been deaf to the response of the onlookers. Now their applause went to her head.

Breaking into a wide grin, she gave a rousing theatrical wave to the group. Then she looked up at Will, her blue-green eyes enormous, as he brought his horse to a halt for their final bow. "Was I really okay?"

Will's blue eyes sparkled. "You were dynamite!" He brushed her lips.

Bree laughed. "Reckon I was pretty good."

Will grinned slyly. "Fearless."

Bree gave an airy wave. "Nothing to it."

"Then you'll be ready to stand in for Maggie again tomorrow."

Bree's blue-green eyes shot up. "Not on your life, cowboy! I've had my moment in the sun. In my case, one moment will suffice."

Will laughed, drawing her more tightly to him. "Well, Bree honey, it was a moment worth seeing. You were spectacular. Correction, tenderfoot—you *are* spectacular." He pressed his mouth to her ear. "Now comes the best part." He reined in his horse as he spoke, then cupped her chin. "The hero's reward—a kiss from his gal. Think you can make this look as real as the rest of your performance?"

Bree laughed softly. "That I can do—spectacularly." Raising her head, she held his gaze for a moment, and then her mouth sought his. Her tongue darted out to wet his lips, then danced back and forth across them until Will let out a low growl and took charge; he possessed her mouth with a lusty assault as he held her head in a firm grip.

Will's kiss sent hot fire through her veins, making her reckless for a moment. She returned his ardor with more intimacy than she would ever have done under public scrutiny. Only the heightened applause and whistles brought her reluctantly to her senses.

Pressing her hands against his chest, she whispered, "Steady, cowboy. This is supposed to be the finale of a family show."

Will's eyes moved over her face with hungry desire; none of the heat subsided from his eyes. His arm tightened around her waist. "Sometimes, tenderfoot, you just don't want to bring that final curtain down."

The next thing Bree knew, Will spurred his stallion forward toward the open barn door and galloped off with her.

"Will, stop!" Bree shouted as he broke the steed into a gallop, raising a cloud of dust that swirled up around the feet of the astonished onlookers. None looked more astonished than Greg Parker.

There was nothing Bree could do but cling to Will as he rode furiously across the plain. Not until they were a good quarter-mile from the barn did Will slow down.

"Will, you're crazy! We can't take off like this. Turn this horse around right this minute!" Bree demanded, knowing even as she spoke that Will had no intention of listening to her. Quite the contrary—the hand gripping her waist slid insolently up her ribcage, and the tips of his fingers trailed the soft roundness of her breast.

"Will," Bree pleaded, warring against the seduction even as his touch intoxicated her, "please go back. I promised I'd get Greg Parker back to Green River to catch a seven o'clock plane. What is he going to think?"

Will pressed her hard against him; she was sharply aware of the powerful muscles of his arms and chest and of his strength and determination and unbridled desire. How was she to act sanely when the feel of him made her more heady than leaping off a thousand roofs onto a thousand horses? The headiness heated her blood until it rushed in her ears, until she didn't want to return any more than Will did.

There was no question in her mind where he was taking her: to the hill where they'd sat this morning loving and warring. At the moment, warring was the last thing on either of their minds.

Will reined his stallion to a halt on a flat clearing at the crest of the hill. They looked out at the breathtakingly beautiful landscape—rugged, stark, and powerful, all ochre, red, and brown. Bree leaned her head back on Will's shoulder; a splendid feeling of awe filled her.

When Will dismounted, he reached up to help Bree off the horse. His hands circled her slim waist. She was more light-headed than she realized; she collapsed breathlessly against him as her feet touched solid ground.

Then she looked up into his laughing eyes. "This is crazy. You know that? What in heaven's name is Greg going to make of this? I didn't even get a chance to ask him what he thought about the show!"

"He thought it was great. Especially"—Will winked

159

—"the new daredevil beauty we just took on. One look at Parker's face and you knew he thought you stole the show."

"I was in no state to look at anyone's face." Bree grinned. "That was the most terrifying experience of my life," she admitted.

Will laughed. "Sorry you went through with it?"

Bree's blue-green eyes sparkled. "Not on your life!"

"Sure you don't want me to tell Maggie when she shows up that we've found ourselves a top-notch replacement?"

"Don't you dare, Will Sheridan!" She grinned. "I'll admit it was exhilarating as well as terrifying. But the exhilaration only hit me after I was safe in your arms."

Smoothing back her hair, Will said softly, "Well now, that's the way it should always be."

His hands moved caressingly across the taut cotton fabric over her breasts.

Bree let out a low, involuntary gasp; his touch sent a shiver of longing through her. "Will, we have to go back in a few minutes. I can't abandon Greg like that. It was a big deal for him to come out here. If he doesn't make that plane, I can forget about getting his help."

Will's hands continued their tender assault. "Someone at the ranch will get him to the airport," he murmured, turning his lips into her thick cinnamon hair.

"But I needed to talk to him. It's important."

Will's lips twisted into the familiar amused curve.

160

"You want to know what's important, Bree honey?" His hand swooped around her neck, and he drew her up so close to him that all Bree could focus on was the sinewy tautness of his body. His other hand skimmed over her breast, up her throat, and then over the lovely line of her jaw. His thumb drew a caressing path across her mouth as his fingers stretched across her face with a touch that was at once tender and assertive. "This is what's important, Bree. This is what counts. Don't you realize that yet?"

His mouth moved over hers, stilling any further protest. Then all thought of protest was erased from Bree's mind as his tongue parted her lips and claimed the velvety moistness of her mouth, nibbling and deliberately teasing. Bree knew that in the end he had a hold over her that was at once arrogant and tender. She surrendered to the assault as shooting spirals of warmth spun through her body.

Bree could feel her whole world shrink until it encompassed only her and Will. The passion of their embrace, the need it generated, made nothing else matter, nothing else exist.

Their kisses grew feverish. Will crushed her against him, and Bree reveled in the feel of the sinewy muscles rippling down his back. His hands ran through her hair, liquid copper in the setting sun.

"Oh, Will," she murmured breathlessly, "make love to me. Make love to me under the open sky."

Everything was right about the moment. Even the usual early evening chill had been replaced by a warm breeze, a harbinger of the coming summer. Bree had never felt so happy. She had been miserable after he'd ridden off this morning, and now here they were, closer than ever. She vowed to be more understanding of Will's feelings about the show, vowed to take things more slowly. They would both compromise. In that moment Bree felt hopeful.

She pressed her lips to the pulse at his throat and breathed in the musk smell of his soap. Will's hands moved in gentle, caressing strokes down her back; each stroke made warmth spread through her until she felt ablaze with it.

He lifted her into his arms, then carried her to a protected spot of soft green grass. When he laid her down, his fingers moved decisively, swiftly, undoing the zipper of her dress. As he slipped the calico costume off her shoulders, his fingers touched her bare skin. Bree shivered, not with cold but with longing and expectation.

After he rid her of her clothes, Bree trembled in delight as his eyes traveled appreciatively down her naked body. He undressed and lay beside her; his mouth once more sought her lips; his tongue explored, plunged, withdrew, and plunged again into the warmth of her mouth. She loved the lean, male feel of him stretched out against her. He lifted her higher, giving his lips access to her rosy-tipped nipples. The tug of his teeth against the buds sent rippling sensations down her body to her very core.

Bree's hands moved freely, lovingly over him. He

was the epitome of maleness: strong, lean, and muscular. Every curve and angle of his body was supremely virile. She pressed hard against him as their lovemaking brought her to unbearable, tingling desire. Her hungry mouth sought his; their moist warmed skin clung. An exquisite timelessness existed between them.

When Will entered her, they sought and found their rhythm easily. Their bodies fit together as if they had been fated to be. Will carried Bree to the brink, holding her there poised. Then, plunging deep inside her, they became one.

Bree stretched out luxuriously against him afterward; a deliciously rich languor overtook her. Will's hand lightly caressed her breasts as she idly ran her fingers through the dark matted hair of his chest. In the crimson glow of the setting sun, neither of them was aware of anything but the magical force that they made together.

They dressed as purple dusk descended. The wind picked up; the leaves of the aspens and cottonwoods rustled overhead. Bree fumbled with her zipper as Will slipped into his shirt. Leaving his shirt unbuttoned, he withdrew her hand and zipped her. Then he turned her around to face him; his head dipped and pressed gently against her lips. His hands stroked her hair. "Well?" He smiled rakishly. "What do you think of making love under open sky, ma'am?"

Bree laughed softly; the corners of her blue-green eyes crinkled. "A rare experience indeed, cowboy."

He caressed her cheek with the back of his hand. "I'd like to make it more frequent."

Bree's breath caught for a moment. "I'd like that too, Will." Her eyes sparkled. "I'd love it."

His brow quirked as he studied her thoughtfully. Bree looked up into his deeply tanned face with its rugged angles and sharp planes.

Her tongue ran over her dry lips. "I want us to be partners, Will." She hesitated. "Partners straight across the board."

He silently traced the curve of her neck with his fingertip. "Well, let's see," he said solemnly.

Bree's brow knitted. Will's ambiguous response wasn't the one she had wanted or expected. A flash of anger darkened her eyes. "I've never proposed to a man before." Her voice held a mixture of outrage and hurt. "Reckon I deserve a better response than the one you just gave me, Will Sheridan."

Will smiled down at her. "There goes that temper of yours again. It was a real nice proposal, Bree honey, one of the nicest I ever did hear," he said with a teasing smile.

"I don't find you very amusing, Will." She eyed him shrewdly. "It's because I own the show, isn't it? That's what galls you."

"Bree, settle down."

"I don't want to settle down. I offered you a partnership, Will. That meant professionally as well as personally. But you can't handle a partnership. Like

Grady said—you don't know the meaning of compromise. You're so caught up in being your own man—"

"Reckon there's only one way to quiet you down, tenderfoot." He swooped her up in his arms and kissed her with almost vengeful intensity. Bree struggled not to give in, but she was lost the moment his lips descended. When at last he broke the kiss, he held her at arm's length; his hands were firmly pressed on her shoulders. "Now, listen here. I love you, Bree. But as for compromise, you don't know the meaning of that word any better than I do."

When Bree started to protest, he placed his hand over her mouth. "I'm not finished. You want it your way, Bree, the same as I want it mine. But whether you own that paper or not, the Sheridan Wild West Show is my baby. I created it, and I've made it into something that matters." He leaned ominously toward her. "It's something I'm proud of, Bree. Just seeing how folks respond to the show makes me feel good inside. I worked too damned hard to get that good feeling to let it slip through my fingers. For any reason —love included." He drew her closer. "Don't you understand, Bree? I don't want to take the show to all corners of the globe. I don't want to travel the world. This is my world. This is where the show belongs." His blue eyes bored into her. "This is where I belong, where I want to be. Either you want to belong here with me or you don't. There's no compromise."

"I do want—"

He pressed his finger to her lips. "You want stardust, not sage dust, Bree honey."

Bree started to argue, but then she shrugged wearily. "I don't really think I know what I want anymore, Will. I thought I knew. I guess I have lived a privileged life. And I guess I can't drop the dream of seeing the Sheridan Wild West Show become the most glamorous entertainment production on both sides of the Pecos." She smiled wanly. "But I do see where you're coming from, Will."

She leaned against the trunk of a willow tree; her eyes studied him with tenderness. "I know you identify strongly with the people who see the show. And that that connection means a great deal to you."

"I see those kids out there in the audience. Some of them look as lost and troubled as I did once upon a time. I try to bring them a little hope, Bree, a little sense of pride. I don't just put on a show for them. I talk to them before and after. I'm living proof to them that you *can* buck the odds. I want to save them from having to find that out the hard way—like I did."

He leaned next to her, shoulder to shoulder. "I had a lot of bitterness in me"—his eyes darkened—"and fear." He laughed dryly. "Tried to drive the fear out by showing everyone I was scared of nothing. I went lookin' for trouble, and I had no trouble finding it."

He closed his eyes for a moment. "When I turned sixteen, I quit school and tracked Grady down. He got the brunt of my bitterness. I guess I held him responsible for everything: for not marrying my mother, for deserting me, for every hurt I ever suffered." He smiled. "He took the abuse for a while. I figured it was because he deserved it. But the truth was, he was just giving me a chance to get it out of my system. Oh, not that he was blameless. But he had offered to marry my mother when he found out she was pregnant."

"And she turned him down?"

He nodded slowly. "She was looking for stardust, too. She was a singer. Had big dreams. Grady wasn't one of them. Even though I'm pretty sure she loved him, she sent him off, and she went after her dream. It wasn't easy for a young woman saddled with a child to make her dream come true." He took a deep breath. Then he stroked Bree's cheek. "Well, she finally did make it out of here. Got her dream." His smile held a hint of bitterness, but then the bitterness faded. "And I've got mine. A good part of it, anyway." He leaned forward and kissed her gently. "Who knows? Maybe I can have it all."

Bree's arms circled his neck. "Who knows, Will? Maybe we both can."

CHAPTER TEN

Maggie McPhee showed up the day before the opening performance at Green River. Everyone breathed a sigh of relief, no one as strongly as Bree.

There was an air of excitement at the ranch as well as at the Green River Fairground, where the tent was being set up. Will had been going down every morning for the previous three days to supervise, but Bree suspected that the real reason he went was to talk to the kids who were hanging out there to get a chance to see him. Although Bree had her hands full, working on new advertising schemes with Greg and arranging additional bookings, she did go down to the fairground with Will a couple of times.

He really was something to see, towering over those kids, his lean, bronzed, ruggedly handsome face smiling down at them. He cut quite a figure in his white cowboy clothes, white suede Stetson, and gleaming tooled-leather boots. Of course it was the six-shooters with their sparkling ivory handles that drew most of the youths' attention. Will always did a few sharpshooting tricks for them, to their awe and great delight.

The kids adored Will. And Bree could see that it wasn't only his rough, tough cowboy appeal that drew them to him. The tenderness and compassion inside him came through as strongly as his masculine image, his self-respect, and his awesome talent.

Watching him, Bree fell in love with Will all over again. And she became doubly determined to make their relationship work. Greg Parker had agreed to handle the advertising campaign, but she had vetoed TV commercials for Will. Somehow Bree doubted that Will would be thrilled to stand naked from the waist up in front of a camera and extol the virtues of a deodorant that a "real man of the West" would use.

For his part, Will was trying, too. He'd consented to taking the show to a few big western cities. And he'd agreed to do a couple of personal appearances. Amazingly, he hadn't even balked too much when the new costumes arrived for the troupe. Will did say they were flashier than he liked, but that was about it. Bree had a feeling his equanimity was largely due to the fact that there'd been no new costume for him in the batch. He assumed that Bree knew when to leave well enough alone; the truth was, the outfit she'd had especially designed for him hadn't arrived yet. She hadn't had the nerve to tell him that it would be here by morning, just in time for the opening at Green River.

Bree was sitting in the little office she'd made for herself at the barn talking on the phone when Annie

Taggart popped her head in. It was eight o'clock; Bree had already been up for several hours.

Bree waved for Annie to come inside, then spoke into the receiver. "You sure you tacked up the whole batch of posters I dropped off?" Pausing for an answer, she gave a thumbs-up sign to Annie. "Terrific. Thanks a lot." She hung up the phone and grinned at Annie. "The new posters finally got here from Greg Parker, and they're up all over Green River advertising the show. We should draw quite a crowd. And so far I've heard from a half-dozen big-city promoters who are going to come out here for tomorrow's opening performance."

Annie leaned against the doorjamb. "Big doings, all right."

"Unless you're hurrying into town," Bree said cheerily, "come and set a spell."

Annie chuckled as she took a seat. "You're gettin' more western every day, gal."

Bree grinned. "I'm feelin' more western every day. There really is a different feeling out here, Annie. Especially being involved in the Wild West show. Every aspect of it is so exciting. I never thought it would be this thrilling—I really didn't." A faint blush colored her cheeks. "I really think things are going to work out all around."

"Well," Annie admitted with a smile, "I never did see Will in a better mood. Then again, I never saw him in love before."

"Never?" Bree asked, once again thinking of that locket in Will's tin.

"Oh, like I said, Will's had his pick of gals over the years. But he's never been serious about any of them. Tell you the truth, I'm real surprised you lassoed him in the way you did, Bree. Never figured Will would lose his heart to anyone. Always seemed to give all of it to the show."

Bree thought she picked up a trace of apprehension in Annie's voice. "What's worrying you, Annie?"

The older women shrugged. "Can't rightly say, exactly. I just hope you ain't thinking you can change Will."

"Change him?" There was an edge to Bree's tone. "A little changing never hurt anyone. I'm changing, after all, and so is Will."

Annie shook her head. "Change has to come from inside, Bree. Forcing it on a person, especially on a man like Will Sheridan—well, gal, all I can say is good luck."

Those words, even the ring of them, gave Bree a disturbing déjà vu feeling. They were the same words Grace had spoken the day Bree had left for Wyoming.

Bree shook herself free of the feeling; a quick, confident smile lit her face. "I think everything's going to work out fine, Annie. You wait and see." She stood up and stretched. Up since five that morning, working at her desk almost the whole time, Bree felt a need for a nice brisk ride. Lately, with Will going into Green

River in the mornings, Bree had taken to riding her steed up into the hills alone.

It wasn't the same as riding with Will, but it was a special time nonetheless. Bree liked the feeling of being alone amid the splendor of the landscape. Alone, and yet not lonely. She got a sense of tranquillity riding up in those hills that she'd never felt in the same way anywhere else.

After Annie left, Bree started for the corral. Along the way she bumped into Grady, who was just coming back from camping out.

"Did you hear? Maggie's back," she told him.

"Not surprised." He grinned.

"Well, I for one am relieved." She and Grady shared a smile, then she glanced up at the overcast sky. "Looks like I still have time for a short ride before it starts to rain. Better to rain today than tomorrow. I'd hate to have to cancel the parade through the fairground before the show." She set her peach-colored felt cowboy hat on her head. It had been a gift from Will. He'd picked it out in Green River especially to complement her cinnamon hair. "Better get going," she said, starting off. She stopped after a few feet and swung around to face Grady. "Hey, you didn't see the new posters Greg Parker did up for the show. There's a couple on my desk. Have a look— they're a real knockout."

Grady rubbed his jaw and watched her go off toward the corral. Then he turned and ambled over to the barn.

Joey was just coming out of Bree's office when Grady walked into the barn. He waved the old man over.

"Did you see this?" Joey asked, holding up a large rolled-up poster. When the old man shook his head, Joey let out a low whistle as he unrolled it for Grady to see.

The old man stared at it quietly and solemnly, absently rubbing at his jaw. Finally he asked, "Will see this yet?"

"Imagine we'd have heard about it loud and clear if he did."

Grady nodded slowly. "Reckon you're right about that." He glanced over his shoulder toward the open barn door. "Looks like a real norther's startin' to brew out there. Yessiree, we're bound for a storm, all right."

Joey gave a nervous laugh. "I see what ya mean, Grady."

Twenty minutes later, Will bounded into Bree's office. He flung open the door and sent it banging into the wall.

The office was empty. As he swirled around, ready to go in search of Bree, Grady appeared at the doorway.

"Where is she?" he demanded hotly.

"Take it easy, boy," Grady cautioned. His eyes fell to the rolled-up poster in Will's tight fist.

Will started past the old man at a stormy pace, but Grady gripped his arm. He was surprisingly strong for his midseventies. "She's not here."

173

"You see this?" Will waved the poster like a weapon.

Grady nodded.

"She's got them plastered up all over town! God knows where else. What the hell is she trying to do?" His tone was low with outrage. "And I was fool enough to think we'd got things straightened out." His knuckles whitened around the poster. "Is she in town?"

"Took off for the hills."

Will shook Grady off and started across the barn.

Grady watched him go off. "Yessiree," he muttered, "gonna be a great stormin' norther, sure as shootin'."

Will had no trouble finding Bree. She was sitting up on the hillside that had become their special place; her horse was grazing lazily nearby.

Her face brightened when she saw Will ride up. She had no premonition of anything being wrong.

As Will reined his horse in, Bree gazed up at him. He looked especially large and powerful astride his steed.

But the way he dismounted made Bree's smile fade swiftly. He got off his horse like a man set for trouble. As he pivoted around to face her fully, she saw the rolled-up poster.

Bree swallowed. "I know what you're going to say, Will. You don't like the poster." She attempted a teasing smile. "Reckon I knew you wouldn't be too keen on it." The smile fell flat.

He took a step toward her; his expression was ominous.

"Come on, Will," Bree cajoled. "It's only a poster." She stepped back. "Personally, I think you look terrific. In fact, that costume they superimposed on you is due to arrive tomorrow. It was supposed to be here before the posters, but—"

"How much you want for me to buy you out?" His cool, steel-edged voice cut through her words.

"Buy me out?"

"You heard me, Bree." He grabbed her roughly by the shoulders. "I want to buy back ownership of the show. How much?"

"I don't understand why you're so all-fired mad."

"You want to know why I'm mad." His mouth cut a tight, thin line. "You make a laughingstock out of me, and you want to know why I'm mad."

"That's ridiculous."

"Ridiculous, huh? I'll tell you what's ridiculous. The way you made me look—sticking that revolting rhinestone-studded circus costume over my photo and plastering it all over town. Even got my poor horse in the same damned matching outfit. The whole town's having a real big laugh over it, but there's one guy not laughing."

"Look, Will"—Bree tried to keep her voice calm— "you needed to spruce up your image. Greg and I—"

"I'll tell you what I need. I need to get my head examined for ever thinking we could see eye to eye. Now, damn it, how much you want?"

Bree bristled. "I don't want to sell. Why'd you ever give up ownership in the first place, anyway?"

"I told you. I needed the money."

"I thought money didn't matter to you," Bree said cuttingly.

"I didn't say the money was for me," Will said curtly.

"Then who was it for?" Bree's eyes narrowed. "That woman whose locket you keep? Was it for her?"

Will laughed coldly. "Not likely." He eyed Bree with a steely gaze. "Not that she wasn't the type to want money like that. But she found someone a long time ago to give her everything she wanted." Will had released Bree and stepped away from her.

Bree took a tentative step toward him. She nodded slowly; the light finally dawned. "Your mother. That's whose photo it is." She touched Will's arm gingerly. "That's who you're talking about. That's right, isn't it?"

Will said nothing at first. There was harshness in his features. "When I saw you that first time, you reminded me of her. It was in your bearing—a regal bearing, even though you were weary and bedraggled. And your eyes—almost the same color. Certainly the same determination."

Will moved away from Bree, as if the nearness itself stirred painful memories.

"She was from the East, too. Came out here when she was nineteen. Had a job singing with a road company of a Broadway show. She met Grady over in

176

Laramie." He laughed dryly. "He was singing country-western songs in some saloon, just for the hell of it. Guess he was good. She thought so, anyway. Had her mind set on the two of them becoming a duet."

Bree smiled faintly. "Reckon he didn't cotton to that idea."

"Hear him tell it, he didn't. But she told me there was a time when the two of them actually did go on the road together. Did a few gigs here and there."

He shook his head, studying Bree almost clinically. "She wanted to make him into something he wasn't. And that's what you're trying to do to me."

Bree shook her head. "No, that's not true. I'm not trying to change you, Will. Not what's inside. It's—it's like an illustrator doing the cover for a book. The artist's job is to make people sit up and take notice of the book. The cover's got to catch the eye. That's all I'm trying to do."

Will gazed at her coolly. "When Grady told my mother he was taking on a cowpunching job in Montana, she walked out on him. She didn't know she was pregnant at the time. But even after she found out, she didn't seek Grady out. He came back to see her a few months later. She couldn't very well hide her condition. He asked her to marry him. But she'd been promised a singing job in a nightclub in Salt Lake City that summer after I was born. She was hoping a talent scout from Vegas would spot her and she'd be on the road to stardom. She tried to talk Grady into auditioning." He laughed dryly, a bitter edge to it. "Grady went back alone to Montana." He paused. "She never did that gig in Salt Lake City. But she finally got what she wanted. When I was thirteen, she was singing in Denver. Turned out the club owner was opening a night spot back east. New York City."

Bree saw a brooding look sweep over his face. "You went?"

Will shook his head. "She went. I refused to go. We fought over it for weeks. Finally she threw up her arms and said she was going without me."

"How could she abandon a thirteen-year-old child?" Bree asked, stunned.

"You'd have to have known her. It wasn't that she didn't want me with her. She just wanted things her way more. And to be fair to her, I guess she thought that after a couple of months I'd change my mind and join her."

"But you didn't," Bree said knowingly.

"She arranged for me to stay with a family she knew. It didn't work out all that well. Summers were better. I worked on ranches around. When I turned sixteen, I quit school and went looking for Grady, as you know. Figured if anyone owed me, he did. Wasn't hard to track him down. A lot of people knew Grady. One day I showed up at the ranch where he was working; next thing I knew, he had me a job there"—a far more tender smile crossed Will's face for a moment—"on condition I go to night school to get my diploma. I put up a fuss, but there are times Grady's even more stubborn than me."

"That's hard to imagine," Bree said softly.

"Then again, there are times I'm more stubborn than him." He paused, seeming to weigh whether he was going to say more. Bree waited, her gaze steady and patient.

Will looked down at her grimly. "I told you before that I sold the ownership of the show because I needed money. It was for Grady. About a year back, he suddenly disappeared. At first I thought he was just off camping, but when a few days passed and he didn't turn up, I was ready to go out scouting for him. That day I get a letter in the mail. From Grady."

"Was he in trouble?" Bree asked.

"He was in trouble all right." Will's voice was husky. "He was dying."

Bree stared at Will, stunned. "Dying?" she echoed.

"Oh, that wasn't what the letter said. But Grady and I could always spot when one of us was trying to lie to the other. He claimed he'd got tired of the show and decided to go back to cowpunching. But I knew how much the show had come to mean to him. I knew what Annie meant to him." He took in a deep breath. "And no matter how much we warred, I knew what I meant to him."

Bree unconsciously gripped Will's arm. "What did you do?"

"I tracked him down again. Only this time it wasn't so easy. He didn't want to be found. Stubborn devil." He sighed. "By the time I got to him, he was in bad

179

shape. Doctor said he needed bypass surgery. Couldn't give any guarantees. But Grady and I'd always bucked the odds before. He was too sick to argue. Didn't find out till he was recovering that I'd sold out to your ex-husband to pay the hospital bills."

Will glanced down at her hand on his arm; then he looked up at her grimly. "Worked out okay all around. Like I said, your ex-husband couldn't have cared less about what we were doing."

"And then I showed up," Bree said in a low voice.

"It's not gonna work, Bree." His tone was so firm and resolute that she suddenly felt frightened.

"Because of some dumb poster?" she asked incredulously.

"Because I've never let a woman ride roughshod over me, and I don't intend to start now." He spoke solemnly, which seemed worse than rage to Bree.

"That's not what I'm trying to do." She felt the color drain from her face. "If this is all about that new outfit I had made for you—"

"Reckon it's the whole principle of the thing, ma'am." His tone was cool and cutting. "I want a price, Bree. I want to buy back my contract."

Bree took a deep breath, trying to still the trembling inside her. "Is that all you want? Or are you saying you want out altogether."

She looked up at him bleakly, but Will's expression was stony. "Go back to New York, Bree. What I can offer you isn't what you want."

180

"Don't tell me what I want!" she shouted, her temper flaring. "Tell me what *you* want."

Will walked over to his horse. With a weary sigh, he mounted. Then he looked down at Bree. "I'll do the show at Green River. I'm not going to let the kids down. But after that, either we work out a deal for me to buy back my contract, or I'm through, Bree. If you want, you can take me to court. They can toss me in jail. I figure either way I'm shackled."

Before Bree could explode, he was off in a cloud of dust. She stared after him; rage gave way to desolation and disbelief.

When the storm erupted, she was still up on the hill, sitting on the grassy knoll in stunned agony. She was oblivious to the rain. Only the whinnying sound of her horse forced her into motion.

As she rode, her anger at Will not only returned, it increased. How could he accuse her of shackling him? How could he tell her to go back to New York? How could he tell her what she wanted and what she didn't want? How could he tell her they were through?

In her mounting fury, Bree paid no attention to the accelerating pace of her horse. And then a bolt of lightning struck. The horse froze, then reared up in panic and bucked furiously.

A cry of terror sprang to Bree's lips. It died in her throat as she was catapulted forward over the steed's head. She flew through the air, only this time there was no one there to catch her; no Will came riding on his great white stallion to grab her up before she was trampled.

She crashed to the hard earth. Terrified, she saw the horse's front hoofs come down over her, but thankfully she blacked out before she felt the impact.

CHAPTER ELEVEN

"Where is she?"

Will looked up from the fire as Grady entered the front door of the ranch. The old man's voice was hoarse with concern.

Will's eyes narrowed. "Isn't she back at the barn?"

Grady shook his head slowly.

The muscle in Will's jaw started to work. "Maybe she headed straight for town."

"She'd have brought her horse back here first," Grady said.

Will knew the old man was right.

Grady kept a steady gaze on him. "We'd better go look for her."

The storm was roaring now. "I'll find her," Will said stonily. "You stay here in case she shows up."

Grady wasn't fooled by Will's cold tone. He could see worry knifing through his boy's heart.

Will threw on a heavy poncho and grabbed up an extra one from the hook by the front door.

Grady's hand reached out, and he pressed it on Will's shoulder. "Be careful."

Will stood as still as a statue for a moment. He closed his eyes. "I left her in a bad state. I told her I wanted out. I told her to go back to New York."

Grady's grip tightened on Will's shoulder. "There are times when a man puts love above all else, son. Above the hurt, the fear, the anger, the bitterness." The old man's smile was gentle. "Reckon we both know that."

Will turned and looked solemnly at his father. And then a tender smile curved his lips. "Reckon you could be right about that . . . Dad."

The norther was a rampaging tempest by the time Will spotted Bree's horse a couple of miles from the hill where he'd left Bree. Panic gripped him. He called out Bree's name. There was no answer. Her horse was terrified, completely spooked by the storm, snorting in panic, rearing and bucking wildly. Will led him to a sheltered spot and began searching on foot for Bree. She had to be somewhere close by. If the storm came before she'd gotten off this hill, either she'd gone to find shelter to wait it out or something terrible had happened to her. Will wanted to think the first, but reason told him Bree would never have just left her horse out in the storm like that.

An hour passed. He was back on his horse, covering first one trail, then the next, calling out Bree's name until he was hoarse. There were so many trails she could have taken. And her horse in his panic could have wandered quite a distance from where he'd left Bree.

Close on the second hour, there was still no sign of her. Will kept searching through the blinding darkness of the storm; the wind screamed and tore at the branches of the aspens and spruces. His panic for her grew with every moment.

He was beginning to fear he'd have to wait for the storm to subside to find Bree when he spotted her mangled hat on the ground, the new one he'd given her just the other day. And then he saw Bree.

He dismounted and rushed to her side. "Bree!" he shouted in agony as he drew her limp body to him.

The moment Dr. Norris of Green River emerged from Will's bedroom, Will sprang to his feet.

"How is she?" he asked anxiously. The rest of the troupe looked on, equally tense.

"Amazing young woman. She's going to be a little sore for a time, but the worst of it is a mild concussion and a couple of bruised ribs. She woke up thinking her horse had trampled her, but she shows no signs of it. Took a pretty bad fall, though. She should stay in bed twenty-four hours, anyway. Better if she stays forty-eight, but she doesn't look the type to take advice. She'll be groggy for a while, but you'll have your hands full keeping her down by morning."

Will started for the door.

The doctor held up his hand.

"I want to see her."

The doctor smiled gently. "She's in a bit of a state right now, and she needs to rest. Why not give it a while?"

Will's eyes narrowed. "You keeping something from me? Are you sure she's all right?"

The doctor bit down on his lip. "Truth is, Will, she doesn't want to talk to you right now. She made that clear. And given the concussion and all, I don't think we want to risk getting her worked up. Fact is, she came to in quite a state of agitation."

"I want to see her—for that very reason," Will said doggedly.

"Will, take my advice—" the doctor started.

"Will has as hard a time taking advice, Doc, as that little gal in his bed," Grady said, smiling.

Grady walked over to Will. "Let me talk to her, son."

Will hesitated. Finally, he nodded.

Ten minutes later, Grady stepped out of the room. Dr. Norris had gone back to town, and the rest of the troupe had returned to the barn. Knowing Bree was all right, they needed to rehearse and then get a good night's rest. They had to be down at the fairground by ten the next morning. The show was set to start with the parade at eleven.

"Well?" Will said, coming to an abrupt halt in his pacing.

"She's asleep now. You better get down to the barn and make sure the rehearsal goes okay. Everyone's kinda upset. I'll stay here in case Bree needs anything."

Will's eyes narrowed. "You talked to her?"

Grady shrugged. "I think she's half delirious, boy. All she said to me was, Tell Will he can't buy back his contract."

"That's it? That's all she said?"

"That's it."

Will finally fell asleep on the couch near three in the morning. Bree had been dozing since late afternoon. Or at least she had been every time Will looked in on her. When he awoke, it was nearly eight. He rose with a start and hurried to the bedroom.

The room was empty.

He came storming into the barn five minutes later. Annie Taggart nearly collided with him.

"Where'd she go now, damn her?" he barked.

"Take it easy. She's with Grady."

"With Grady where?"

Annie shrugged. "All I know is, Grady said you're to meet him at the fairground at nine."

Will glared at her. "What's going on?"

Annie sighed. "You'll have to ask Grady. At the fairground."

There wasn't much Will could do but head on down to Green River. He needed to be there early anyway to make sure there were no last-minute details that hadn't been attended to.

When he drove down Main Street in Green River,

Will noticed that all the new posters were down. The ones he'd originally had done at Van's were all up in their place.

The same was true at the fairground. A large crowd had already gathered, and Will was bombarded by people as soon as he was spotted. Grady came to his rescue, shouting to the crowd that Will had to get ready for the show.

Grady led Will to the huge tepee-shaped show tent with SHERIDAN WILD WEST SHOW emblazoned across the top. As they neared the entrance, Will snapped, "Where is she?"

Grady didn't answer, but when he opened the front flap of the tent and gave Will a gentle shove inside, he didn't follow after him.

Will started to turn, and then he saw Bree emerge from the stage set saloon. She was wearing an outfit straight out of frontier days—a simple blue-and-pink calico skirt and a high-necked, mutton-sleeved pale pink blouse.

Will walked slowly over to her and came to a halt a few feet away.

Bree smiled tentatively. "I reckon, cowboy, that what you told me once is true. When it comes right down to it"—she closed the distance between them—"a woman's got to believe in her man." She tilted her head up to him. "I believe in you, Will. And just so you don't ever have to worry about my trying to ride roughshod over you ever again—"

"Bree, wait. I'm sorry. It's just—well, you do get to me, tenderfoot."

Bree's eyes sparkled. "Reckon you have the same effect on me." Then without another word she withdrew a sheaf of folded papers from one deep pocket of her skirt and one of Will's six-shooters from the other. Then she shoved the gun into his hand, pivoted around, and stepped back twenty paces.

She held the folded papers in her outstretched hand. "Okay, cowboy. This here's my ownership papers for the Sheridan Wild West Show. Let's see how good a shot you are."

Will's eyes narrowed. "You sure you know what you're doing?"

"I'm sure I love you, Will. I don't have much else to offer you than that, but everything I do have is yours."

Will's aim was perfect. The bullet hole was dead center. Then just for good measure, Bree tore the papers into confetti and tossed them into the air.

Will swept her up into his arms, and they kissed passionately.

"Take me up to our hill," she whispered.

"The show—"

"You've got close to an hour."

"You're in no condition, Bree honey."

"Are you going to spend the rest of your life arguing with me, cowboy?"

Will grinned. "Reckon I am—if you'll let me, ma'am."

The warmth of the sun caressed them as they sat astride Will's horse looking out over the hillside. Bree rested her head on Will's shoulder and sighed happily as he stroked her hair.

In the distance stretched the amber hills, dotted with columbines, asters, and wildflowers of every color. The sky was the bluest Bree could ever remember seeing, with nary a cloud to mar it. Beyond, the Rocky Mountains rose proud and majestic. Like this land. Like Will.

Bree drank in the sweet, fresh air. Then she tilted her head up to Will's, and he circled his arms around her waist, one hand lightly on the reins.

He lowered his mouth to hers; his blue eyes were tender and luminous. His kiss was infinitely gentle. Then his lips lightly brushed every precious feature of her face—her eyes, her nose, her chin, and her soft cinnamon hair.

Bree smiled at him, a smile full of joy and promise.

Will stroked her cheek with the back of his hand. "Reckon I better take you back home," he said softly, gently pressing the heels of his boots into the horse's flanks.

"After the show," Bree said.

"You're in no condition—"

"I'm not missing the show."

"Oh, yes you are."

"No use arguing with me."

"Bree—"

"Will—"

Their soft laughter filtered through the hillside.

"About that costume, Will . . ."

Silence.

"Okay, Will, forget the dumb costume."

"Bree?"

"Yes, Will?"

"I love you, ma'am."

"I love you, cowboy."